RECALLING MY DEMON

POSSESSIVELOVE

COLETTE DAVISON

To Jess,
With Love,
Colette Davison

POSSESSIVE LOVE

RECALLING MY DEMON

I'm told Nethermire House is haunted, but the truth is even stranger.

Nethermire is home to an eccentric 80-year-old and the young man she claims is her great-nephew.

Except he's not.

He's a demon.

Brin's chaotic, bratty ways draw me to him. When he calls me Daddy, I'm a goner. I want to protect him, take care of him, and call him mine.

But when he gets taken to hell, our happiness is shattered.

Can I recall him to my side, or will I lose him forever?

Recalling My Demon is a standalone MM paranormal romance in the *Possessive Love* multi-author series. It has an age-gap relationship between a bratty demon who needs someone to love him more than he realises and an ex-priest who's now a Daddy.

To all my readers.
You are amazing exactly as you are.

"Morning, Ian, I'm afraid you've drawn the short straw today, love."

I pause on my way to the coffee machine and stare at Nora, the practice manager. "The short straw?"

"She's sending you to the haunted house," Angela says.

Like me, Angela is a district nurse, but she's been working for the practice a lot longer, despite being ten years my junior.

Nora tuts. "Ignore her. Nethermire's not haunted."

"Been there, have you?" Angela asks.

"Well, no, but ghosts don't exist."

"You keep telling yourself that. Make me a coffee, would you, Ian?"

"Does anyone else want one?"

Nora shakes her head.

"Martha Edwards lives at Nethermire House," Angela says as I make coffee. "She's sweet enough, although she'll talk your ear off if you give her half the chance. She's in her eighties and lives in that big old house by herself. We do regular welfare checks. If you ask me, she'd be better off in a care home. I have no idea how she manages the house on her own."

"Is she ill?" I ask.

"Fit as a fiddle."

I hand Angela a mug of coffee. "Why do you say the house is haunted?"

She shudders. "Because it is. Just driving through the gates gives me the creeps. I get full-body shivers like someone's walked over my grave. And once you're inside, it's like you're being watched. Sometimes I hear laughter."

"Laughter?" I sip my coffee. I haven't worked at the practice long, but I hadn't taken Angela for being the imaginative type.

"Do you believe in ghosts? What's the church's stance on that sort of thing?"

I stare at my black coffee. "I'm not part of the church anymore."

"Martha will keep you there all day with her chatter if she could," Nora says. "Or all night if it's your last call. My advice? Make it your first call, and then you've got an excuse to leave."

"She's lonely," Angela says.

"Even though she has ghosts for company?" I ask.

Angela rolls her eyes. "Now you're teasing me."

I chuckle. "I'm sorry."

"Like hell you are." She presses her fingers over her lips. "Sorry. I shouldn't say things like that in front of you, as you're a priest and all. You'll have me saying Hail Marys or something."

"Ex-priest."

"These are your patient lists for the day," Nora says. "Get to as many as you can and let me know if there's any you won't make so I can give them a call and bump them to another day."

I scan my list as I drink my coffee. I recognise a few patients, but the rest are new to me. In time, I'll get to know everyone who needs regular home visits.

"I'm off," Angela says. "Have a good day." She pauses in the doorway. "Make sure you go to Nethermire before dark."

"Why?"

"You don't want to get trapped in a haunted house after dark. That's when ghosts are more powerful."

"Um, I'm not sure that's true."

She wags her finger. "You'll be singing a different tune when I see you tomorrow morning. Maybe you should take a cross or something."

"That's for vampires."

"Surely, the cross would ward against all things unholy? Do you have any holy water left from your time in the church?"

"The house freaks you out, doesn't it?"

"That's putting it mildly. Take care."

I wash our coffee mugs, make sure my nursing bag is stocked, and then go to my car. It's a pre-loved banger, but it gets me from A to B. I put the postcode for Nethermire House into Google Maps on my phone and pull out of the car park. I may as well do it first, out of curiosity, if nothing else.

I enjoy talking to people. As a district nurse, I spend more time with patients than I would if I were in clinics all day. Even so, it's rarely long enough.

An electronic voice directs me out of the town and into the countryside, down narrow, winding roads lined with hedges and tall trees. It would look nicer in summer. The dark, twisting branches are ominous as they reach into the grey sky like bony fingers. Now my imagination is running riot. Thank you, Angela.

I'm taken down a tiny side road to a wrought-iron gate. A red brick wall surrounds the perimeter of the grounds. The height of the wall and a screen of trees hide the house. I get out and try the gate. It's locked, but there's a security intercom. It's old, with a single button and a speaker. I press the white button. I'm about to give up waiting when the speaker crackles.

"Hello?" The weathered voice is feminine. I assume it's Martha Edwards.

"Hi. My name's Ian Watts. I'm one of the district nurses. You should be expecting me?"

"I've not met you before."

"No. I'm fairly new to the practice. Would you prefer a female nurse?" Some patients do.

She chuckles. "No, no. You'll do fine. I'll open the gate."

The intercom fizzes and falls silent. The gates open with a whine. I get back in my car. A shiver snakes through my body as I drive through the gate. Why did I listen to Angela's tall tales? I'm too old for ghosts and fairy tales.

The drive is covered in autumn leaves. Grass pushes up through a myriad of cracks. I gasp as the house comes into view. It's not a mansion, but it's not far off. It's a double-fronted red brick building. Windows in the roof suggest the house has attic rooms. The windows on the ground and first floors are tall and in a Gothic style. A green-framed morning room, with coloured glass in the top panes of each window, is attached to the left of the house. The door is green but in dire need of a fresh coat of paint. I jog up the stone steps to it and raise my hand to knock. The door opens before I can.

"Well, aren't you tall?" A woman smiles at me.

She's shorter than I am, her back bent with age. She leans on a walking stick. Her face is wrinkled, her skin crinkled like ageing paper. She's wearing a touch of make-up, red lipstick and some blusher. Her white hair is braided and pinned around the crown of her head.

"Martha Edwards?"

"Who else would I be? Come in. Come in." She turns and shuffles into the house.

The hall has a beautiful floor tiled in a flower pattern. A dark wood staircase leads upstairs. Martha takes me into a reception room with red velvet curtains and gold wallpaper. The furniture looks as old as the house. The hearth is the most imposing feature in the room. The mantle is chocolate-brown marble. Red brick surrounds the fire-place, in which a fierce fire burns. It's not warm outside, but the heat from the fire makes me too hot. An overwhelming sense of being watched prickles my skin. It's ridiculous. Martha and I are alone in the room and, presumably, the house.

"Would you like a cuppa?" Martha asks, gesturing for me to sit.

"No, I'm fine."

"Nonsense. Let me get you something. A nice cup of sweet tea and a biscuit."

"If I had tea and biscuits at every house call, I'd need new trousers by the end of the week."

She laughs and sits. "Point taken. What should I call you? Nurse Watts? Nurse Ian?"

"Ian is fine."

"It's the first time they've sent a male nurse. It's wonderful more men are getting into the profession." She glances at a portrait on the wall of a young woman in Victorian clothing. "In my grandmother's day, nursing was purely for women."

Despite Martha's age, the family resemblance between her and the portrait is clear. It must be of her grandmother.

"Luckily, times have changed since then," I say.

"Hm. So they have."

"Was your grandmother a nurse?"

"For a short while. What made you go into nursing?"

"I want to help people."

"And do you get to do that?"

"Yes."

"Have you been doing it long?" She peers at me. "You have grey in your hair. You must be what? Forty? Forty-five?"

I shouldn't answer. We're not supposed to give out personal information, even something as simple as our age. I smile and nod, not committing to a specific number. I check her notes.

"Have you had any falls recently?"

She shakes her head.

"How are you coping with your arthritis?"

She shrugs. "The same as ever. My joints ache more in this weather." She gestures at the fire. "Heat helps." Her gaze lingers on the flickering flames, which reflect in her bright blue eyes. Her smile becomes soft and—grateful.

"Do you have someone to help with the house?"

"Hm? Oh, yes, my nephew comes to visit from time to time. No. Not today."

I frown. "Sorry?"

She tears her gaze from the fire. "My nephew. He *won't* be visiting today."

A log in the fire pops and cracks, making me jump. I swear the intensity of the flames has increased, even though no extra fuel has been added.

"Tsk," Martha mutters under her breath.

"Are you scolding me?"

"Oh, no, of course not. It's getting a little too hot in here, don't you think?" She looks pointedly at the fire.

"Would you like me to douse the flames?"

She waves her hands. "No, no. There's no need. They'll quiet down on their own. What else do you need to ask?"

I run through some welfare questions, including ones to assess her memory and her mental health. Depression and loneliness can go hand in hand. The last thing I do is take her blood pressure, which hasn't changed since Angela was here last. By the time I'm done, the fire is much smaller than it was.

"I must say, you're a lot more relaxed than the nurse who normally comes," Martha says as I put the blood pressure cuff away.

"Angela?"

"Yes. She barely stays for five minutes. Can't wait to get out of here."

"We have different styles."

"Well, I like your style, Ian. You can come again."

"Is there anything else you need while I'm here?"

"No. I'm fine. I've enjoyed your company, but I know you must be busy, so I'll let you get on."

The fire blazes briefly as though a gust of wind has swept down the chimney. A glance out the window is enough to tell me there is no breeze.

Martha glares at the fireplace. "Unless you'd like that cuppa before you go?"

"No, thank you."

"Maybe next time. You should come at the end of your day. Then you'd have more time to chat."

"I'll have to see how it goes. You were on my way to another call this morning." Which isn't true at all. None of my other calls are anywhere near Nethermire House.

"Let me see you out."

"There's no need."

She rolls her eyes. "I'm not an invalid yet, young man." She uses her cane to help her stand. "I can still be a good host."

I follow her to the front door.

"Come again," she says cheerfully.

I wave as I make my way down the steps to my car. She stands on the top step, watching me until I'm safely inside it. Then she goes inside and shuts the door. I put the next address into Google Maps and then turn the engine on. As I pull away from the house, I glance at it one last time. Martha is in the window. I slam my foot on the brake. The car screeches to a halt. Is there someone behind her? A shadowy figure? I blink. Martha is alone. My imagination is playing tricks on me. Nethermire isn't haunted. It can't be.

I step out of the fire, which dies down to embers in an instant, and reform my body as I stand behind Mother at the window. I duck back, out of sight, as Nurse Ian looks right at me. His car comes to a sudden stop. Mother stays still until the car has driven down the drive. Then she sighs and shakes her head.

"What?" I ask, spreading my arms wide.

She turns to me and puts her hand on my cheek. "I love you, Brin, but you must learn to be more subtle. You also need to learn patience."

"I'm patient. Impatient would have been showing myself while he was here and telling him how sexy he is."

Mother laughs and sits. "You thought he was attractive?"

I kneel beside her and scrunch my face as I recall Ian's. "Sexy, yes."

He has a weathered face etched with kindness. Dark eyes and hair with hints of grey peppered through it. His jaw is steeply angled, his chin broad. He sports a beard and moustache, the hair on his chin as white as Mother's, save for right beneath his lower lip, where darker hair stubbornly clings on. The hair covering his upper lip and jaw is darker, though more streaked with grey than that on his head. He's tall and broad, and although his uniform and jacket hid his physique, I imagine strong, well-defined muscles. I could be making that last part up.

"I want him. Do you think he might want me?"

Mother strokes my black hair away from my face. "You'll have to ask him."

"I would have, but you made it clear I wasn't allowed to."

"How would I have explained the fire dying down to nothing in an instant?"

I shrug.

She curses under her breath. "I should have told him you were my great-nephew."

"Nephew. Great-nephew. What's the difference?"

"A generation."

"Mother is much easier to remember than aunt or great-aunt."

"I know. But I'm too old to be your mother."

"Um. But you are my mother."

"No one is going to believe I have a twenty-three-year-old son."

"Except I'm not—"

She puts her fingers over my lips. "You look twenty-three, and that's all that matters." She moves her fingers away.

I pout.

"Next time he comes, feel free to visit your great-aunt. Make sure you disguise yourself, though." She runs her hand over my left horn.

"I hate having to hide." I half close my eyes and concentrate on changing my form anyway.

It's a strange sensation. Not painful but not pleasant either. I'm rearranging myself, hiding all my demonic features. My horns, ears, wings, tail, and the true colour of my eyes.

I need to practice maintaining a human form. It's a concentration game, which is exhausting and hard when I'm distracted. I've discovered that sex is distracting but so much fun. My eyes always slip first, so after freaking one guy out so much he ran out of the house naked, I've learnt not to face men during sex. It makes it no less fun and gives me a chance to reassert my human appearance before my hook-up notices my eyes have become red.

Thankfully, when it's only me and Mother at home—which is most of the time—I can look like my true self.

I tilt my head. "Better."

She sighs and nods, sadness flooding her eyes. "I hate that you have to hide. One day, you'll find someone you can trust with your true form."

"Like Father trusted you?"

"Yes."

I stand and cross to the window. Nurse Ian is long gone. Tyre tracks are the only reminder he was ever here. They're deeper where he stopped suddenly.

"He's gorgeous," I whisper.

I doubt I'll ever find someone like Mother. My interactions with people are limited to the guys I invite over, using hook-up apps. I'm not naive enough to believe that any of those one-night stands will lead me to a man I can trust with my secret. Which is fine. I don't need anyone else in my life I can confide in. I have Mother. She keeps me safe. Men are for fun. I capture my bottom lip between my teeth. What are the chances that Nurse Ian will want to have fun with me?

"He seemed kind," Mother says. "He wasn't checking his watch every few seconds like he was desperate to leave."

"He looked strong."

"There's more to people than looks."

"I know. But looks are all I'm interested in."

I sit on the floor beside Mother, rest my chin on her knees, and stare up at her. "Do you still like it here after all these years?"

"I love this house. But it's bricks and mortar. You're the reason I stay."

"The house is my whole world, but you could have more."

She taps my nose. "The house and the garden."

"It's a big garden."

"It is. I don't want more, Brin. I have everything I need right here."

"Except Father."

She sighs and looks away. "He's gone, Brin."

I don't remember him, but talking about him makes Mother sad. "I'm sorry for mentioning him."

"It's fine, sweetheart. I miss him every day, but I've accepted that he can't return to us. Now, will you accompany me on a walk around the garden? I need to shore up our defences."

"Of course."

She leans on me rather than her walking stick. We go to the cardinal and intercardinal points of the garden. At each one, Mother traces the shape of a sigil onto the brick wall and speaks words in Latin. She's tried to teach them to me, but they flutter out of my mind. They're impossible to grasp hold of. Impossible to remember. Impossible to understand. Mother says they keep me safe, and I believe her.

"Done." Her face is paler than when she started, and the bags under her eyes are more pronounced.

"You need to rest."

She pats my hand. "I will, sweetheart. Will you take me to my room?"

I help her from the garden to her room on the first floor. Her gait is unsteady and slow. I hate that she has to tire herself out because of me. She settles in bed, and I tuck the quilt around her.

"I'll go and get your walking stick, so it's here when you need it."

"Thank you. You're such a good boy. What will you do while I rest?"

I grin. "I'll think of something. I'm good at entertaining myself."

Sadness manifests on her face. "I wish you didn't have to."

I lean down and kiss her forehead. "I don't mind. Sleep well."

I jog downstairs to retrieve her walking stick. By the time I return to her room, she's asleep. Her breathing is soft. I sit beside her for a while, watching the rise and fall of her chest. Mother is the only family I've ever known. The only family I need. Yet unlike me, she keeps getting older. I can light a fire, turn myself into flames, and hide my demonic appearance, but what good is any of that if I can't stop time from attacking her?

Angela thrusts a mug into my hand the moment I walk into the staff room. "I made you a coffee."

"What do you want?"

She gasps. "Can't I do something nice for you without wanting anything?"

"You can, but you never have. You normally get me to make you a coffee."

"That's not true."

I chuckle. "It is, but I figured it was some kind of rite of passage, given that I'm the new guy." I raise the mug in thanks and then sip the dark liquid. "Thanks for the coffee."

I pick up my roster for the day, intending on perusing it while enjoying my coffee, and sit at the wonky round table.

Angela sidles up to me. "How's your day looking?"

"Busy as ever. Why?"

"Just wondering." She sits opposite me and twiddles her thumbs.

"Uh-huh. What do you want, Angela?"

"Martha Edwards is on my list, and I was wondering if you'd swap with me. I'll take two of your patients off your hands." She speaks in a rush.

"Why?"

"The house freaks me out, but you haven't said a word about it since you visited. So I assumed you didn't sense a strange presence."

Except I did.

She arches an eyebrow. "Did you?"

I drum my fingers on the table. "No." Did my voice squeak? Damn. It did.

"Maybe you should offer to do an exorcism on the house."

"I couldn't, even if Martha wanted me to."

"Because you're not a priest anymore?"

"Because I'm not an exorcist."

She stares at me. "Can't any priest do it?"

"No. Each diocese has a specially trained exorcist."

Her mouth falls open. "Well, you learn something new every day, don't you?" She clasps her hands in a pleading gesture and tucks them beneath her chin. "Will you swap with me? Please?"

I shift in my chair. I could say no. I should say no. Although Martha Edwards is lovely, Nethermire House is an unsettling place. It's been three weeks since I visited, and I haven't been able to shake the sensation of being watched. Sometimes I relive the moment I saw the figure behind Martha in my dreams. I must have imagined it, but the rational part of my brain doesn't want to function when it comes to that house.

And yet I'm certain Angela will be in and out in the blink of an eye. Martha Edwards deserves better care than that.

I sigh. "Fine. I'll swap with you. But I get to choose which patients of mine you get."

She extends her hand. "Deal."

We shake on it, and I pick two patients Angela will get along with. A quick visit to Nora gets our lists updated, and we set off to start our days.

I go to Nethermire House first. I'd rather visit while the sun is out than later in the day when the light is fading. I can only imagine that Nethermire will seem creepier after dark.

As before, it takes Martha a while to answer the intercom. "Ian, I'm so glad it's you. Do come in."

The gate opens with a whine. I drive through, shuddering as I did before, like someone has walked over my grave.

Martha is waiting for me on the doorstep, leaning on her walking stick and smiling cheerfully.

"You look well," I say.

"I'm feeling just peachy today. Thank you for asking. Do come in. I've made tea."

She takes me into the same room as before. A tray with a china teapot sits on the coffee table. Steam rises out of the spout. A matching plate sits beside it, with delicate cakes and biscuits arranged neatly. How did she know when to make the tea? How did she get the tray in here when she uses a walking stick? I glance around, but there's no sign of a trolley.

"Are you expecting someone?"

"Only you, dear. Oh, and my grand-nephew promised to visit today. He's a lovely young man." She sits and pours two cups of tea. "Milk? Sugar?"

"As it comes, thanks." I'd decline, but she's already gone to the trouble of making it. "You haven't lit a fire today."

"No need. The sun is shining, and it's a cheerful day. I'll light one later if it gets chilly."

The room is less oppressive than the last time I was here. My skin isn't crawling, and I don't feel like I'm being watched. More proof I imagined it during my first visit. I should know better than to allow tall tales to creep me out.

"It's good your nephew and grand-nephew are able to visit you."

"Nephew? Oh. Silly me. I meant grand-nephew last time you were here. I get my words muddled sometimes." She wags her finger at me. "Don't go writing that down. My mind is as sharp as it's always been."

I chuckle. "I don't doubt it." I sip the tea. It's a good brew, not so-called builder's tea, and it's at a perfect drinking temperature.

"Have a cake or a biscuit. I put them out especially for you."

"I'm sorry. How did you know when someone would call?"

"You're here at the same time as last time. My assumption is I'm first on the list. Someone always comes early, around this time. Of course I could have been wrong, and then the tea would have gone to waste, but I wasn't, was I?"

Her smile is cheerful, yet it makes me shiver, even though her assumption was one hundred per cent correct and no doubt based on months, if not years, of experience with district nurses coming to check on her.

A loud chime ding-dongs in the hallway. It's a doorbell you'd expect to hear in a period movie.

"That will be Brin."

"Would you like me to let him in?" I ask as she reaches for her walking stick.

"Oh, would you? That would be most kind. You are a lovely man, Ian."

I glance out the window as I stand. My car is the only one in the driveway. "How did he get here?"

"There's a bus stop not far from the end of the lane."

I frown. I haven't been here long. Surely, I would have passed her grand-nephew on the lane if he'd walked here?

"There's a footpath through the woods," Martha says. "It's much more direct than the lane."

Is it me, or does Martha Edwards have an answer for everything? Answers which make perfect sense and which I need to accept. No more jumping at shadows.

Not wanting to keep her grand-nephew waiting any longer, I hurry to the front door and open it. My jaw practically hits the floor as

I come face to face with a stunning young man with jet-black hair and warm, tawny, flawless skin. His eyes are such a dark shade of brown it's almost impossible to tell where his pupils end and his irises begin. He's wearing a worn leather jacket, faded black jeans, and a mottled dark grey T-shirt. His bottom lip is thick, perfect for pouting.

"Nurse Ian." He raises his thick, dark brows a fraction, his eyes sparkling as he smirks. "Mo—Martha has told me all about you." His voice is soft, light, and playful.

"You're her grand-nephew?"

"Brin." He flicks his gaze over me. "You are gorgeous."

I take a half step back. "Uh—"

"I shouldn't have said that, should I?" He runs his thumb over his bottom lip. "I'd apologise, except it's true. Hm, you are one gorgeous man."

So is he. I swallow, needing to maintain my composure and remain professional. "Martha is through here." I gesture to the lounge.

"She likes that room. Have you seen the rest of the house? I could give you a tour."

"No, I haven't."

Brin flounces into the house, kicks his boots off, and wanders into the lounge. I follow in his wake. He leans down to kiss his great-aunt on the forehead, grabs a cake off the plate, and sits in a chair with one leg looped over the arm. He peels the case away from the cake and takes a big bite. Crumbs drop onto his chin, so he flicks his tongue out to lick them off.

"Ian is here to do my welfare check," Martha explains.

"I guessed." Brin stares at me as he devours the rest of the cake.

I can't take my eyes off him.

"Don't let me stop you from doing your job. I love watching a man in uniform work." He winks.

"You'll have to forgive him. My grand-nephew is a terrible flirt," Martha says.

I scrabble to get the blood pressure monitor out of my bag and kneel beside Martha.

"A man in uniform on his knees. Sexy."

"Brin," Martha says, her tone not as sharp and short as I'd expect for a true admonishment.

"What? It's true."

I put the cuff around Martha's arm and turn the monitor on. "Do you live nearby?" I ask Brin.

"Close enough to visit whenever I want."

"He's a good boy," Martha says. "He often helps around the house. I don't know what I'd do without him." She looks at him with a fondness that makes my heart melt.

"Try not to talk so I can get an accurate reading."

"Sorry."

I restart the monitor, paying close attention to the figures rather than how Brin leans forward to pluck another cake from the plate. I certainly don't watch the way his white teeth sink into the cake or the way he licks the pale crumbs from his lips.

I record the figures and put the monitor away. "Same as last time, so no concerns there."

I run through my welfare questions, stumbling over my words, even though I know the questions by heart. Martha answers each one cheerfully, allowing me time to add to my notes.

"All done for this visit." I stand, fully intending to leave.

"You haven't finished your tea," Martha says, gesturing to the half-drunk cup.

"It's probably cold by now."

Brin jumps up and picks the cup up, cradling it in his hands for a moment before handing it to me. "Try it."

I'm careful not to let our fingers brush as I take the cup and taste the tea. It's still a perfect drinking temperature, even though it was poured half an hour ago.

"You should try a cake too." Brin selects one and holds it out. "Martha is excellent at baking."

"You made these?" I'm talking to Martha but can't tear my gaze away from Brin's eyes. His smirk is hypnotic too.

"Yes," she replies.

Brin peels the case away and lifts the cake to my lips. I should take it from him, but instead, I open my lips and nibble the cake. It's moist, rich, and sweet, with a strong hint of vanilla.

"It's good. Compliments to the chef."

"You've made a mess, Nurse Ian." Brin uses his thumb to wipe crumbs and a touch of icing off my beard. He puts his finger into his mouth and sucks on it. "All clean."

I shiver. "I should go."

"So soon?"

I was right. His lips are perfect for pouting.

"Yes, I've got other patients to see."

"Of course. Ian is a busy man, Brin. Would you be a dear and see him out for me?" Martha asks.

"If I must."

I trip over my feet as I follow Brin to the door. He opens it and tilts his head, his stare so intense I wouldn't be surprised if he were looking into my soul.

"I enjoyed meeting you, Nurse Ian."

I nod, not trusting myself to speak.

"I'm here a lot, so I'm sure we'll see each other again."

"I'm sure we will. Goodbye."

I stumble down the steps to my car. Brin leans against the door frame, arms loosely folded, watching me as I get into my car and fasten my seat belt. I've never been attracted to men significantly younger than me, but I can't deny that he is beautiful or that my body is crying out to respond to his unbridled flirting.

I won't.

I can't.

Martha is my patient, and Brin—Brin is—.

I shake my head and drive.

"Hi, sexy," I say as I open the door.

Ian looks as gorgeous as the last two times I saw him. He's utterly swoon-worthy, but I can't tell if he's interested in me. I'm not good at reading humans, probably due to my lack of interaction with them. Hook-up apps are so much easier. Guys on those don't get affronted when I tell them how beautiful they are and ask them to fuck me senseless.

Mother left the gate open so Ian could drive in whenever he arrived. Thankfully, the wards she's placed on the house and grounds aren't dependent on whether or not the gate is open or closed. No demon can walk in or out, even through the open gate. I should know. I've tried.

"I'm afraid Mo—Martha is sleeping right now."

I need to get better at not calling her Mother in front of Ian. Another problem I don't have when I summon a man via a hook-up app. They come late after she's in bed, and the house is big enough that she'd never hear us anyway. She knows, of course. I wouldn't invite anyone into the house without her permission.

"Oh. Well, I can put her on the list for tomorrow," Ian says.

"Or you could come in for a few minutes. She might wake up soon. I'm sure I can entertain you."

Ian clears his throat. "That's okay. I'll come back tomorrow."

I pout. This isn't going well. Am I coming on too strong? I wouldn't know how to rein myself in even if I tried. Should I be honest with him?

"You're hot, and I want you to fuck me."

Ian widens his eyes. His lips part into an O.

"Too forward?"

He rakes his hand through his mostly dark hair. "While that's good to know, I'm working."

"You could come back after work. I'll be here." I'm always here. "Or, you know, you could come in, and I could suck your cock while you wait for Mo—Martha to wake."

He takes two steps backwards. "I'll come back tomorrow."

This is going terribly. What's a socially incompetent demon supposed to do to get the man of his wet dreams?

"I'm sorry. I'm coming on too strong. Can we start over?" I give Ian what I hope is a sweet smile.

He moves forward. "Does this approach normally work for you?"

"Asking someone if they'll fuck me?"

"Yes."

"Uh, yes, when I do it via an app."

He rubs the back of his neck. "A hook-up app?"

I nod.

"All people are looking for on those apps is sex," he says.

"I know."

"But we haven't met via an app."

"No, but isn't being upfront and honest a good thing? You're sexy, so if you're attracted to me too, why shouldn't we have sex?"

He chuckles. "You're—"

"I'm what? I'm not your patient. I'm not registered at your—your—surgery?" I shouldn't have phrased that as a question.

"It doesn't change the fact I'm working."

"But you won't be later." I bat my lashes. Girls do it all the time in the movies. Surely, it's a trick that will work for a guy too. "Wait. If that's your objection, it must mean you like me." I move closer. "Do you like me?"

"I—" He raises his hands as though he's going to clasp my shoulders before dropping them to his sides again. "I should go. Tell your great-aunt I'll be back tomorrow."

How can I save this? Can I save this? "Don't go."

"I have other patients to see."

I can't save this, so why stop? "All right. For what it's worth, it's hot that you're so dedicated to your patients." I step into his personal space and look up into his eyes. "You're big, strong, and caring, all wrapped up in a handsome package. I bet a man like you would be able to teach me a thing or two."

Ian's pupils shrink. "What could I teach you?"

"Plenty. Like how to flirt." I wink, spin away, and lean against the doorframe with my arms loosely folded. "How a man like you fucks."

"How old are you? Twenty? Twenty-two?"

"I'm older than I look. Old enough to know what I want. Old enough to enjoy a pounding from a man like you. Come over later. Show me how good a teacher you are."

"I'm a nurse. Not a teacher."

"I would love to play doctors and nurses with you. You can examine me whenever you want, Nurse Ian."

He wipes his hand over his face. "You're—"

"A handful?"

"Yes. I'll come back tomorrow. To see Martha."

I press my hand over my heart. "You wound me. I don't think I'll ever recover from this rejection."

He rolls his eyes. "You'll cope. If sex is all you want, you can use that app you mentioned."

"Are you on the app?"

"No. And even if I was, I wouldn't tell you what my profile is. It wouldn't be professional."

"Why not? Is there a rule that says you can't fuck your patient's grand-nephew?"

He sighs and straightens. "Not that I know of."

"Then, if you like me, be naughty with me. Or teach me how not to be naughty. Either, or. As long as sex is involved. I'm easy."

"I noticed. I'll be back tomorrow."

"You keep saying that, yet you're still standing here."

The vein in Ian's neck throbs. "I'm going." He doesn't move.

"Come inside. Let me suck you off. It would be our secret. No one would know."

He makes a strangled noise. Is he thinking about it?

"I'll stop if you tell me to. Give me the order, and I'll try to be good."

"If I—? Order—? Try—?" His brown eyes lose focus.

"Do you know what I think?"

"What?"

"You like me being naughty."

"I—?" He shakes his head. "I'm going."

I arch an eyebrow. "Are you?"

"Yes."

I look pointedly at his feet, which aren't moving.

He shakes himself, turns, and strides to his car. He opens the door, but instead of getting inside, he looks at me. "I'll—"

"Come back tomorrow to see Martha. I'll tell her."

"Thank you. I might see you then."

"I don't have to be here. If you don't want me to be." I'll be here, but I can avoid him by hanging out in the extensive gardens or turning to flames in one of the house's many hearths.

"I wouldn't ask you to stay away on my account."

Does that mean he likes me? At the very least, he doesn't hate me. Maybe he could help me.

I ruffle my hair. Not being able to touch my hard, twisting horns doesn't feel right. "In all seriousness, there is something you might be able to teach me. If you're game."

Ian leans on the car door. "You weren't being serious before?"

"I was, but this request has nothing to do with sex. Promise."

"I'm listening."

"As you've probably guessed, I'm not very good with people. I— had a sheltered upbringing. Very sheltered. I still don't get out much."

"Except to visit your great-aunt."

"Yeah. Exactly. So anyway, could you teach me how to behave? Around people. I'm not being suggestive. At all."

Ian's smile makes me weak at the knees. "Wouldn't you be better off socialising with people closer to your own age?"

I purse my lips. "No. I don't think that's a good idea."

"Why?"

Good question. "You'll have more experience than guys in their twenties. More life experience. More people experience. You could come here one evening and teach me how to have a normal conversation. Without sex talk. There won't be any of that."

"Why here?"

"Oh, um, it's a beautiful house. And the grounds are gorgeous. I still haven't given you that tour. I know you need to get to your next patient, but I'll show you around. Next time. If you want."

"No flirting?"

"None. I promise." Did I sound solemn enough?

He taps the car door. "Let me think about it." It's not a no.

"All right."

"I'll see your aunt tomorrow. And you, if you're here."

"I will be." I wave as he gets in the car.

He pulls away, glancing at me in his mirrors more than once.

CHAPTER
FIVE
IAN

Why do I leave my visit to Nethermire until the end of the day?

Brin.

He's the reason. I shouldn't be attracted to him or tempted to accept his sexual advances. He's twenty years my junior. At least. He's not even my type. Yet something about his chaotic forthrightness captivates me and makes me forget how spooky the house was the first time I was there. I want to learn more about him. He said he had a sheltered upbringing, which I can well believe based on his clumsy attempts to get me into bed. Yet he seems far from inexperienced. Then again, I've had my fair share of hook-ups. Flirting and conversation aren't necessities. Even foreplay can often fall by the wayside as the urgent need to fornicate takes over.

He opens the door as soon as I get out of the car. "Hello, Nurse Ian."

He's wearing a tight-fitting black T-shirt and black skinny jeans. His feet are bare. It seems too cold for that. Damn, his smirk is sexy. He takes my breath away, as though I'm seeing and appreciating him for the first time. My pulse picks up, making me glad my work uniform is fairly baggy.

"Brin. Is Martha awake?"

"Yes. She's in the lounge. She's made tea."

I wince. "I hope she didn't go to that trouble this morning."

"No. She had a feeling you'd come late today. Is this your last appointment?"

Say no. Say no. "Yes."

Brin's eyes gleam. "So you won't be rushing off afterwards?"

"I still have paperwork to complete."

"Can it wait?"

He must have been moving closer as we've been talking. He's right in front of me now, close enough to touch. Close enough to pull into my arms and kiss. Are his lips as good for kissing as they are for pouting? I need to stop thinking this way. I'm working. He's too young. He's stunning.

"You promised there would be no flirting," I remind him in an authoritative tone.

He gasps. "I'm not flirting."

"This is you not flirting?"

"Absolutely. Cross my heart." He does so. "And in the interests of not flirting, I could give you a tour of the house and grounds after you've seen Martha."

I swallow.

"Did you think about my request?"

"Your—"

Brin giggles. "I asked if you could teach me how to be better at conversation."

"Conversation that doesn't involve sex talk or flirting."

He tilts his chin up and looks me in the eyes. "Yes. Will you?"

I clear my throat. "The tea will be getting cold."

"You're right. We should go inside. After you." He steps aside.

My gaze lingers on him until I've passed him.

I go to the lounge, the only room in the house I've seen. Martha is sitting in the same armchair as always. She smiles brightly as I enter and gestures to the tray of tea and cakes.

"I'm so sorry you had a wasted trip yesterday," she says.

I sit in the chair adjacent to her. Brin follows me into the room and pours me and Martha tea. Once he's handed us our cups, he sits cross-legged on the floor beneath the tall, Gothic window, even though there are plenty more seats.

"No need to apologise. I hope you're all right."

"I am. I'm at an age where I need naps from time to time."

I sip the tea, expecting it to be cold. Once again, it's the perfect drinking temperature. How did Martha know when to prepare tea for? I glance around the room, my stare finally falling on the fireplace. Logs are stacked in it, ready to be lit.

"Is something the matter?" Martha asks.

"No."

"Brin told me you and he had a nice chat yesterday. I hope he didn't keep you too long."

"Not at all." I peek at him, even though I shouldn't.

I'm not surprised to find him smirking, his stare fixed on me. It's getting dark, but there's enough light streaming through the window to create a curtain around him, enhancing his beauty. I look away before I salivate. He's too young. He's my patient's relative.

"Shall we get started?" I ask.

"Of course. I know all the questions you're going to ask off by heart by now."

I chuckle. "I'm sure you do."

It doesn't take me long to run through the welfare questions and check her blood pressure. It's a little lower than three weeks ago, so I make a note to talk to one of the doctors when I'm in the surgery in the morning. It's something we should keep an eye on.

"All done." I pack my things away.

"Do you need to rush off?" Martha asks.

I wasn't lying when I told Brin I had paperwork to do. Or, more accurately, visit notes to put on the computer system at the surgery. But I could do it in the morning before I go on visits. I usually do. All that awaits me is dinner for one and whatever is on the TV.

I should go. I have no reason to stay. Brin is here to keep Martha company; every second I spend near him is dangerous. Compared to yesterday, he's being well behaved.

Teach me how not to be naughty.

I shiver. I want to, more than I should.

"I can stay, but not for long."

Martha smiles. "Long enough to finish your tea and have a cake or two?"

"I can manage that." What am I doing?

"How long have you been a nurse?"

"I've been qualified for three years."

Martha raises her eyebrows. "That surprises me. I imagined it would have been your calling. You seem like the kind of man who wants to take care of people." She glances at Brin.

"Which is why I went into nursing." I've told her too much already. I'm not about to let any more personal details slip.

"Do you enjoy it?"

"Yes."

"That's good. Hopefully, you'll be sticking around here for a while then. You're so much warmer than that other nurse. Angela. That's her name, isn't it, Brin?"

"Yes."

"And the other nurse who used to come before you was even worse. She'd tremble like a leaf the whole time she was here and be out the door within five minutes flat. What was her name, Brin?"

"Beth."

"There's a rumour Nethermire House is haunted," I say.

Martha widens her eyes. "Well, that explains it. It's nonsense, of course. There are no ghosts here." She peers at me. "You don't think it's haunted, do you?"

Brin stretches his legs out and leans back onto his hands, his head cocked as he and his great-aunt wait for me to respond.

"The house can be a little unsettling."

"In what way?" Martha asks.

"The first time I was here, I felt like I was being watched."

"Watched?" Brin jumps to his feet. "By what?"

I glance at the fire. "I don't know. I also thought I saw someone at the window as I left. Standing behind you, Martha. But whatever it was vanished in the blink of an eye."

"I've lived here my whole life. This house is not haunted," Martha says.

I put my hands up. "I believe you. I haven't felt or seen anything since my first visit. I put it down to being spooked by rumours."

"As you should." She yawns. "I'm feeling a little tired. Brin, sweetheart, could you help me to my room?"

"Of course." He hurries to her side and helps her stand. He picks up her walking stick as she leans on him.

"You don't need to leave," Martha says. "Finish your tea and the cakes."

I should go, but I stay where I am as Brin guides Martha out of the room. The stairs creak in their wake, as do the floorboards above my head, lending weight to the haunted house theory. And yet, if it were haunted, Martha would know about it.

I stand and cross to the fireplace, crouching before it. I run my hands over the marble and stone and lean inside and look up the chimney. Nothing seems amiss or out of place. Yet it was the source of that unsettling sensation of being watched.

"I can light it if you want."

I jump out of my skin and fall onto my arse at the sound of Brin's voice. He's lounging against the doorframe.

"I didn't hear you come in." Or walk down the creaky stairs, for that matter. "Is Martha all right?"

"Yes. She's asleep. Probably will be for an hour or two."

"Will you stay?"

"Yes. Will you?"

I hesitate. I should go.

"You never answered my question."

"Your—question—?"

Teach me how not to be naughty.

He doesn't mean that question.

"Will I teach you the art of conversation?"

"Yes."

"I don't think it's a good idea, Brin." If I spend time with him, how long will I be able to resist him?

He pouts. Why did he have to pout? I want to stride over there and kiss his pout away or teach him not to be a brat. I shiver. I love a brat, but the ones I seek out are older than Brin, closer to my own age.

"Back to plan A?" he asks.

"What's plan A?" I can guess the answer.

He grins. "Sex." He lifts his T-shirt high enough to reveal a sliver of tummy flesh and then puts the tips of his fingers beneath the waistband of his black jeans. "If you want me, you can have me."

I do want him, even though I shouldn't. I glance up at the ceiling.

"This is a big house. We can go to a room far away from Martha's. She won't hear a thing."

I stand. "You're a brat."

"Is that a compliment?"

I chuckle. "No. I'm not going to sleep with you, Brin."

He rolls his eyes and sighs. "You can't blame me for trying. But I can take a hint." He pulls his T-shirt down and then picks up the tray. "See yourself out." He strides out of the room.

I follow him. I shouldn't, but I do. He's already going into a doorway down the hall as I step out of the lounge. I jog after him into what turns out to be a kitchen. I stop and stare. It's like I've walked into a time warp. Either that or the kitchen has been transported straight out of a period drama, complete with a range cooker, cast-iron pans hanging on the wall, and a drying rack suspended from the ceiling.

Brin puts the tray beside a huge ceramic sink, and leans against the wooden worktop. "I thought you were leaving?"

"Do you want me to?"

"No, but I don't understand why you're still here. You won't teach me how to talk to people, and you won't fuck me either. So, why are you here, Nurse Ian?"

"You don't need to call me that."

He folds his arms and tilts his hips. "What should I call you?"

Daddy? "Ian." My throat is dry.

"Why are you still here, Ian?" My name has never sounded so sexy.

My pulse picks up. "I should go." My voice is huskier and lower than normal.

"If you want to."

I move towards him, my body at odds with my head.

"Are you still working?" he asks.

"No."

"I'm not your patient."

"No." I'm right in front of him, our bodies almost touching.

"I want you. Do you want me?"

"You're too young."

He throws his head back and laughs. "I told you. I'm not as young as I look. I'm old enough to be naughty with you, Ian. Old enough to know what I want." He pushes away from the work surface and presses against my chest. "Old enough to want you." He puts his hands on my hips and pulls my groin against him.

Blood rushes to my cock, which plumps up.

"You're so big and strong." He licks his lips. "You like taking care of people, don't you?"

"Yes."

He caresses my chest through my uniform. "Like taking care of men."

"Yes." My voice has a growly edge.

"I bet you're good at it." He walks his fingers up my chest to cup and caress my bearded jaw. "Is there another name you like the men you fuck to call you? If so, tell me what it is."

How does he know? I shut my eyes and breathe slowly. He doesn't know. He's guessing. He's seducing me. He's succeeding.

"Tell me what to call you," he whispers. "Tell me what name turns you on."

"Daddy." I shouldn't have admitted that to him, of all people. But I can't take my truth back.

"Daddy?"

I shiver and open my eyes to meet his stare.

"Yes, I can see that." He pushes onto his toes and nibbles my jaw. "You want me, don't you, Daddy?"

"Yes."

He sinks to the soles of his feet, puts his hand on my nape, and pulls my head down until our lips are a breath apart. "Then take me, Daddy. Please?"

I an closes the tiny gap between us to claim my lips. I gasp at the fervour with which he kisses me. He sucks on my lower lip, his teeth gently nipping it before running his tongue along it. I take the hint and part my lips, welcoming his tongue into my mouth. I groan and tilt my head back so he can kiss me deeper. His beard tickles and scrapes my skin. He puts his hands on my hips and pushes my T-shirt up so he can touch me.

"You're such a good kisser, Daddy," I whisper as he relents to breathe. Calling someone Daddy is a new experience for me, but it feels right.

He kisses me again, harder and deeper. My toes curl. I whimper and moan as his tongue explores my mouth and caresses mine. He reaches behind me. There's a clink and clatter. Is he pushing the tray away? He grips my hips, lifts me, and sits me on the edge of the work-top. He knocks my knees apart and steps between them, his chest pressed to mine as he moves my T-shirt to stroke my back and rests his other hand against my nape. I yank his top up to explore his furry chest with my hands.

He breaks the kiss and, breathing hard, rests his forehead against mine. He brushes his thumb back and forth behind my ear. "You are such a naughty boy."

"Me?" I use my most innocent voice.

"Yes." He growls and nips my lower lip again. "You're very naughty."

"I did ask you to teach me to be good."

"That's not what you said."

"Isn't it?"

"You asked me to teach you how not to be naughty."

"Hm, isn't that the same thing?"

"No."

"I also asked you to be naughty with me."

He chuckles. "Yes, you did."

"We're both being naughty."

"We are."

He glances up.

"She can't hear. But if you're worried about getting caught, we can go somewhere else."

"Where?"

"Let me down, and I'll show you."

He steps back, allowing me to hop off the counter. I almost take his hand but decide against it. I leave the kitchen at a brisk walk, not looking back to ensure he's following me. He will if he wants me. If he's changed his mind, he'll leave.

I go across the hall and open a door into a second reception room situated behind the first. I flick the light on. Not that it's very bright. All the furniture is covered in white sheets. The heavy curtains are closed. Wood is stacked in the fireplace, ready to be lit.

Ian puts his hands on my waist from behind and kisses my neck.

"Martha doesn't use this room anymore," I say.

"How big is this house?"

"Four reception rooms and the sunroom downstairs, and ten bedrooms upstairs."

"Wow." He slips his fingers beneath the waistband of my jeans. Is he going to touch my cock?

I lean against his chest and thrust my hips into his touch.

"Eager boy."

Boy. Daddy. Words I've never associated with sex before, but they're turning me on. I push back and rub my arse over his crotch. His cock is delightfully hard.

"You are such a needy, demanding boy."

"Are you complaining?"

He chuckles before nipping and licking my neck. "No." He holds my throat loosely, not applying any pressure.

I whimper and tip my head back. "I want you, Daddy."

His cock jerks against my arse. He lets out a low, rumbling noise, which makes his chest reverberate against my back. He pushes me towards and around the sofa, spins me around, wraps his arms around me, and pitches us onto it. I spread my legs to allow him to settle between them. He kisses me hard, his hands running through my hair. What would it feel like to have him touch my horns?

I snap my eyes shut as my control over my human form wavers. I need to get a grip, which is hard when Ian is kissing my neck and rubbing his crotch against mine. Why are we still wearing clothes?

"You okay?" he asks.

"Yes." Once I'm sure I'm not going to betray myself, I open my eyes and smile. "You were going to fuck me, Daddy."

Regret floods his eyes. "I don't bring lube and condoms to work."

I have both in my room. I can't admit it. Ian thinks I don't live here. I don't even need to use condoms. I'm immune to human illnesses and diseases. I can't catch them and can't pass them on, but I can't share that information with Ian either.

"But we can still have fun." He kneels up and undoes my jeans.

I lift my hips as he yanks my jeans below my arse. "No underwear?"

I grin. "Less to take off."

"You are such a naughty boy." He kisses me and strokes my length.

I groan as he applies the perfect pressure to drive me insane. "I want you to come too."

His navy-blue trousers have a catch rather than a button, so they're easy to undo. He's wearing underwear, but I make short work of pushing both garments to his knees so I can feast my gaze on his hard, thick cock. I whimper. I'm not going to get the pleasure of having it inside me.

He lies over me and frots against me, his lips hungrily devouring mine. The friction of his cock rubbing over mine is amazing, but being face to face is too dangerous. What if I lose control again? What if he sees the true colour of my eyes?

I push him away a fraction, stopping him from kissing me. "Can we—? Can I—?" I make a turning motion with my hand.

Ian frowns and sits upright, giving me the freedom to turn over and push onto my hands and knees.

"I can't fuck you, boy."

"You can rub your cock between my arse cheeks, Daddy."

He sucks in a breath.

I look at him over my shoulder and waggle my eyebrows. "Not quite as good, but it'll be fun."

He strokes his cock a few times, generating pre-cum, which he smears over my arse crack.

"Pleasure yourself, boy."

I grasp my cock and masturbate while he holds his cock and rubs the tip and length between my arse cheeks. The damp head of his cock brushes over my arse hole on each stroke. Why can't he throw caution to the wind and push inside me? I want him so badly.

"That feels so good, Daddy."

"I've never done this before."

"Is it fun for you too?"

"Yes, boy." He grunts and groans as he picks up the pace, thrusting faster and faster between my arse cheeks.

Between the sensation of his hard dick against my arse hole and the way I'm frantically rubbing myself off, I'm beside myself with need. My balls are heavy, and pressure bears down on my groin.

"Daddy, I—" I gasp and whimper as my orgasm hits me, my body shuddering with the exertion of emptying my load onto the sheet-covered sofa.

I can tell the moment my eyes revert to their normal appearance. It's okay. He can't see my face. I fight to get control back, but Ian is driving me wild with the speed at which he's rocking his hips. Damn, his hard cock feels amazing as it moves between my arse cheeks over and over.

He cries out. Hot cum spurts over my crack and lower back. He collapses on me, kissing my back as his furry chest heaves against me.

"Turn around so I can hold you, boy."

I shake my head and press my face against the sofa. I'm not in control yet. I can't let him see my face.

"What's wrong, boy?"

"Nothing, Daddy. I'm happy, that's all."

"You don't regret it, do you?" His voice quivers.

"No. No. Not all. It was fun and wonderful and—"

I want to turn around and wrap my arms around him, but I can't. Not yet. I have to concentrate on my appearance, not the thud of his heart against my back, his cock pressing against my arse, his hot cum sandwiched between us, or the way my insides are fluttering because he wants to hug me.

I'm used to guys who fuck and roll away. It suits me fine. I've never needed or wanted after-sex cuddles. Being abandoned within seconds gives me the space and time to ensure my appearance doesn't betray me. Those men were happy to leave without a word or even a kiss goodbye.

But Ian isn't moving except to kiss and stroke me. It's scary.

Eventually, I'm able to make my eyes human and dark once more. I wriggle underneath him, turning so we're chest to chest. He smiles and stares into my eyes before kissing me tenderly on the lips.

The stairs creak.

"Fuck." He scrambles off me and pulls his underpants and trousers up.

"Martha won't come in here."

He holds out his hand. I accept it, letting him help me up. He uses the corner of the sheet to clean me up and then pulls my jeans up and fastens them. He pushes my hair back, cups my cheeks, and kisses me.

"I had fun, boy."

"So did I. Daddy."

He kisses me again and then slips out of the room. I slump onto the sofa. Ian's and Mother's voices drift through the house, loud enough to be recognisable, too quiet for me to make out what they're saying. The front door bangs shut. It's old and heavy, so it's impossible to close it quietly. He's probably in his car now, driving away. I shouldn't care. I'm used to men fucking and running. I've always wanted them to go. Maintaining a human form is so damned exhausting.

This time, my chest aches. I touch my lips, remembering the way he kissed me. What's wrong with me?

The door opens, and Mother shuffles into the room.

"Are you all right, Brin?"

I nod and release my concentration, allowing my body to morph back into its true form.

She sits beside me. "Are you sure?"

"Yes." I lean my head on her shoulder. "He wanted me."

"I guessed." She puts her hand on my knee and squeezes. "He's a nice man. You should see him again."

"Again? Oh, you mean when he comes to see you?"

"I rather thought he might come to see you."

"Why?"

"Because he likes you."

"He wanted sex. We both wanted sex."

"But not more?"

I shake my head.

"Are you sure?"

No.

"What's wrong, Brin?" She strokes my hair.

"I lied to him."

"That's never bothered you before."

"I know. And it shouldn't bother me now. It's not as if I can tell him what I am. Thanks for the sex. By the way, I'm a demon. Want to do it again?"

Mother chuckles. "Well, I wouldn't put it so bluntly."

I pull away from her. "I won't see him again anyway."

"You can if you want to."

"I don't." My voice is rough. "We had fun together. Now it's over. The same as every other man I've been with. I don't need more. I don't want more."

"Brin—"

"I don't."

I made lots of mistakes yesterday, not least of which was scurrying out of Nethermire House like a teenager who had been caught with his pants down. I'm forty-five. I shouldn't be embarrassed about having sex with another adult. But when the cloud of lust passed, I was left with the stark reminder that Brin is at least twenty years my junior. Twenty years. What could someone so young, vibrant, and sexy possibly see in a man my age?

Does Brin think all I wanted was to fuck and run? Not that he said or did anything to suggest he wanted more than one quick encounter. Not that I gave him the chance. I left without any promises of wanting more. I'm an arsehole, which is why I'm driving to Netherfield on my day off. One of my other mistakes? Not asking Brin for any way to contact him. His phone number. His address. Nor did I give him a way to contact me. Will he be visiting his great-aunt today? Perhaps not, but maybe she'll give me his phone number.

I stop in front of the gate but don't get out of the car to ring the buzzer. Should I be here? What right do I have to intrude on Martha's day? None, but I owe Brin—something. An explanation. A conversation to discover if either of us wants more. Do I want more? He's so young, yet while I was holding, kissing, and touching him, he made me feel more alive than I have in years. And when he called me Daddy—

I shiver. He didn't question or baulk at my request. He embraced it. Does he know about Daddy kink? Is it something he's into, or did he entertain my whims in order to seduce me? Not that I didn't want him. Once he'd batted away all my reservations, my mind was willing to follow wherever my desire led.

Something knocks against my window. I jump and hit my head on the roof of the car. I press my hand to my chest and look for the source of the noise. A man wearing mostly black is bending down and peering at me. His face is pale and gaunt, his chin sharp, his lips thin. His eyes have a cold sparkle as he smiles and gestures for me to wind the window down.

"I didn't mean to scare you. Do you know the owner?" He gestures to the gate.

Goosebumps break out over my arms.

"Would you be able to tell me their name? Perhaps give me some contact details? I'm wondering if the house is for sale, you see."

"If it were, there would be a For Sale sign."

He chuckles. "Sometimes all it takes is a little nudge for someone to realise they want to sell." He curls his fingers over the bottom edge of the window. "If nothing else, I'd like to be able to sit down with the owner and talk to them about the house. Perhaps they could come to the gate for a chat. You could facilitate that, couldn't you?"

"No. I'm not here to visit." Why am I lying to him? "I'm lost, but I know where to go now. Would you mind?"

"Of course." He pulls his hands away and stands, his motions slow. "It was nice making your acquaintance. Perhaps our paths will cross again."

"I doubt that." I wind the window up and put the car into reverse.

The man doesn't move as I back down the lane to a point wide enough to turn. I glance in my rear-view mirror. He's still standing in front of the gate, watching me as I drive away.

I can't exactly drive around the block, so I navigate country lanes for a good half hour, getting lost before finding my way back to roads I recognise, eventually ending up in front of Nethermire House once more.

The man has gone. Why did he give me the creeps? It was probably the smarmy, patronising manner in which he spoke.

I get out of the car and ring the buzzer, unsurprised when it takes Martha a while to respond.

"Hello?"

"Hi, Martha, it's Ian. Nurse Ian. Could I—? Would you mind if —?" What am I doing here?

"Ian. I wasn't expecting you. Did you forget something yesterday?"

"No. It's not a work call. I'm off duty."

"Ah. Brin isn't here."

"That's not—"

She cuts me off with a chuckle. "Why you're here? It is. Come inside. I'll put some tea on."

A few minutes later, I'm sitting in Martha's front parlour with a cuppa, which is the perfect drinking temperature. The fireplace is set but not lit. The house seems quieter than the last few times I visited, probably because Brin isn't here, but at least I don't feel like I'm being watched.

"You came to see Brin," Martha says.

"I—" I'm back to feeling like a teenager who's been caught doing something he shouldn't. "I need to talk to him."

Martha stares at the fireplace. "I'll let him know."

"Is there any chance you could give me his phone number? Then I wouldn't have to use you as the middleman."

"I don't mind. It's nice to have a visitor. I don't see many people except you and Brin."

"You don't have any other family close by?"

"No."

Which means Brin doesn't either.

"Did you have children of your own?"

She smiles and sips her tea. I guess that means it's none of my business. Which it isn't. What am I doing here?

I finish my tea and put the cup on the tray. "Would you pass my number on to Brin?" I glance around for something to write it on.

"In the kitchen. To the left of the sink. Third drawer down."

"Thank you."

I wander down the hall to the kitchen but don't go inside. My stare snags on the door to the reception room Brin and I fooled around in yesterday evening. The memory replays in my mind in glorious technicolour and surround sound. The feel of his soft, flawless skin. The taste of his luscious, pouty lips. The husky quality of his voice as he called me Daddy, as he whimpered, gasped, and groaned while I thrust my cock between his arse cheeks. Oh, how I would have loved to enter him, to feel the hot pulse of his arse around my cock. I still want that and more besides.

Paper. I need to get paper. I turn my back on the room and go into the kitchen. It's empty and cold. Frowning, I touch the tip of one finger against the range cooker. It has no warmth at all. I thought they were supposed to be kept on all the time. At least, that's what they say in those programmes where people want to find homes in the country. I look around, but there isn't a modern electric kettle. How did Martha heat the water for the tea?

I find paper and a pen in the drawer Martha told me to look in, write my phone number down, and tear the paper off. I put everything away and then hurry back to the front reception room. A creak from upstairs stops me in my tracks. My heart thuds. I stare up the stairs, listening. Silence responds.

"Hello?"

Nothing.

"I'm in here, dear," Martha says from the doorway.

"I thought I heard someone upstairs."

"I'm here alone, aside from you."

I hand her the paper with my phone number on it.

"I'll be sure Brin gets it."

"Thank you. Oh, before I go, there was a man outside the gate earlier."

"A man?"

"Yes. He said he was interested in buying the house or talking to you about it. He wanted your name and number. I didn't give him either."

Martha stiffens. Her walking stick rattles against the floor. "Did he say who he was?"

"No. Has he bothered you before?"

She smiles, but it seems forced. "No. If you see him again, tell him the house isn't for sale and that it never will be and that, no, I don't wish to talk to him or anyone else about it."

"I will. Would you tell Brin I'm sorry for dashing off yesterday?"

"Of course." She touches my hand. "He doesn't think he can have a man like you."

I crumple my brow. "What do you mean?"

She chuckles. "Nothing. I'm a doting great-aunt who wants only the best for Brin. He's a lonely soul, though he'll fiercely deny it. He needs someone in his life he can trust. Someone besides me. Can he trust you, Ian?"

Trust me to do what?

"Ignore me. More ramblings of an old woman. Will you stay for more tea?"

"Thank you, but no."

"I suppose you have things to do. A handsome young man like you must be busy. It was nice of you to take time out of your day to come and see Brin. I'm sorry you missed him. You must like him."

"I—do. He's—" What words can I use to describe Brin? I sigh. "Younger than me. A lot younger than me."

"I was a lot younger than my lover."

"You—what?"

"He was the epitome of tall, dark, and handsome. He swept me off my feet with a charming smile." Her eyes become distant and watery. She holds her hand out as though reaching out to the spectre of him. "We spent many happy years together, so don't let a little thing like age bother you. What matters is what the heart wants. But you're probably not thinking with your heart yet, are you?" She winks.

I squirm.

"Don't answer that." Her expression falls. "I miss him."

"Your lover?"

"Yes. Mal."

"You never married?"

"Oh, heavens no. Marriage wasn't possible. Besides, we were happy."

"What happened?"

"He was imprisoned. Years ago now, but I still think about him."

"Can't you visit him?"

"No, dear. He's beyond my reach." She sighs. "I don't think my heart will ever forget him. Love. It's a blessing and a curse. It brings us happiness and sorrow in equal measure."

"I've never—"

"Been in love? That's a shame. There's nothing like it. For all the pain I feel now, I wouldn't give up even a second of the time I spent with Mal. I'm sorry. I'm keeping you from your day."

"Not at all." Listening to her talk is fascinating.

She waves the piece of paper. "I'll give this to Brin."

"Thank you."

She sees me to the door. A crow caws in the garden, drawing my attention in that direction.

"You can explore the garden if you want. I'm afraid it's too big to show you around." She lifts her walking stick.

"Brin said he'd give me a tour." Assuming I ever see him again.

"Well, if you have the time and inclination now, feel free to look around yourself. You never know what you might find. The gate will be open when you're ready to leave."

"You wouldn't mind?"

"Of course not. Have fun." Her eyes twinkle as she shoves me out the door.

I turn. "I forgot."

She raises her eyebrows.

"Your range cooker was cold. I thought they had to stay lit?"

"They do. Don't worry. Brin will light it for me when he visits."

"But—"

"Bye, Ian. Enjoy the garden." She shuts the door in my face.

She must have wanted to be rid of me. I glance at my car, but my stare is drawn back to the garden. It's as creepy as the house, full of overgrown grass, wildflowers, trees, and all manner of places to hide in. Yet I'm drawn to it. Or maybe I'm not ready to leave. Maybe I'm hoping if I linger long enough, Brin will arrive, and I'll get to explain myself.

"He came back, Brin. To see you," Mother says as I join her in the front reception room.

I roll my eyes. "You don't have to gloat. The cooker is lit. Sorry I let it go out." I heard most of her conversation with Ian while I was 'skulking around upstairs', as Mother would put it. Not all of it, but enough.

"He's in the garden. You should join him."

"Why?"

"He likes you, and you like him. He came back."

"You already said that."

"He's a good man."

"We're not going to fall in love and live happily ever after. I want to— He wants to— You know."

She chuckles. "I do know. And you'll never know what might be unless you go and talk to him."

"You told him I wasn't here."

"I'm sure you can come up with something."

I look away. What's another lie? The growing pile of lies is precisely why I can't have more than one-off sex with Ian or anyone. I don't want to have to keep lying, which is crazy. I'm a demon.

Shouldn't I thrive on lies and deceit? Only, I'm half-human too. Not that humans don't lie. They do. If TV shows, movies, and video games are anything to go by, they lie a lot.

"Talk to him," Mother says. "Or— You know."

"My mother, the enabler."

"Why shouldn't you have fun if you both want to?"

Why shouldn't we? Because he doesn't know what I am. Because I'm tired of pretending. Tired of hiding. I want someone to desire the real me, not run screaming for the hills. But in lieu of that fantasy ever becoming a reality, another round with Ian would be fun.

"Fine. I'll go talk to him." I kiss her before heading for the door.

She clears her throat, stopping me. Ah, yes. I can't find Ian looking like this. I concentrate on shifting my form, ridding myself of my demonic features so only a human remains. Mother's expression is sad, but she nods, smiles, and makes a shooing motion.

I find Ian at the far end of the garden, looking at a wooden archway which stands beside a dilapidated greenhouse.

"The garden's seen better days," I say.

He gasps and turns. "Brin."

"Sorry. I didn't mean to scare you. Martha said you were here, so I thought I'd come and find you."

He comes closer, his boots scrunching across the grass. "I'm the one who should be apologising."

"For visiting?"

"For yesterday."

"You're sorry for not quite screwing me?"

He chuckles. "No. I very much enjoyed that. I'm sorry for leaving the way I did."

I shrug. "It's what the guys I meet through that app do, so I wasn't surprised."

He shivers and pulls his coat tight. "It's getting chilly out here." He looks me up and down. "Aren't you freezing? You're not wearing a coat."

"I'm fine." I could warm him if he knew what I was.

He comes closer still and cups my cheek. "You're warm."

"And your hand is cold."

He snatches it away. "Sorry. I am sorry, Brin. Just because men have treated you that way in the past doesn't make it right for me to do the same thing. I don't normally fuck and run."

"Oh? Do tell. What is Nurse Ian's MO?"

"I like to spend time cuddling before falling asleep. When we wake, I make us breakfast."

"You like to take care of the people you fuck?"

"Yes."

"Is that why you like to be called Daddy during sex?"

His cheeks flush red. "Have you heard of Daddy kink?"

"No. Educate me." I gesture towards a stone bench and then sit on it.

Ian joins me. "It's a sexual fetish. I enjoy taking on a Dominant role during sex. I take charge, while the person I'm with is submissive."

"And calls you Daddy?"

"Yes."

"It turns you on?"

"Yes." His voice has become husky.

"And you call them boy?"

"Or girl."

I arch an eyebrow. "You're bi?"

"Yes."

I hook my elbows over the back of the bench and cross one knee over the other. "Another one of Nurse Ian's secrets is revealed."

"It's hardly a secret."

"I didn't know."

"You didn't ask." His voice has become authoritative.

"Being a Daddy is more than a pet name, isn't it?"

"Yes. As a Daddy, I want to take care of my partner. Protect them, nurture them, but also discipline them if they need it."

"And how would you discipline a naughty boy like me?"

He smirks. "That depends."

"On?"

"His limits. But if he were open to it, I'd bend him over my knee and spank his arse until he was sorry."

My stomach flutters. "I've never been spanked before. Would you spank me if I'm naughty?"

He leans towards me until I can feel his breath on my face. "If?"

I laugh. "When." I bite my lip and look away. I have enough trouble maintaining my human form when I orgasm. Would I be able to while being spanked? Something tells me the experience would be sensual as well as painful. "Why did you come back?"

"To apologise."

"You've done that. Not that you needed to. Why are you still here?"

"Because we're talking. And I think we're flirting."

"You think?"

"It felt like we were, but you seem to have gone cold. I like you, Brin. I enjoyed being close yesterday. But if all you wanted was a one and done, say so, and I'll go."

I bow my head. "It's all I've ever had before."

"But is it all you want?"

I clench my hands. "What exactly are you offering me? Sex followed by cuddles, falling asleep together, waking up in each other's arms? I don't do romantic shit like that." I stand, put several paces between us, and hug myself. I can't do romantic stuff like that, because I wouldn't be able to maintain this form. "I enjoy sex, Ian. That's all. So if you want to bend me over the bench and pound my arse, feel free. If you want romance and a relationship, I'm not your guy."

His footsteps get closer. His shadow falls over me, large and strangely comforting. He puts his hands on my hips and leans down to kiss my neck. I tilt my head to the side, giving him better access, and close my eyes. His lips are warm and soft against my skin. He's so good at kissing. So good at turning me into a needy mess. I want him even more than the first time I saw him. He's everything I didn't know I needed.

"How long have you been into Daddy kink?" Why am I asking that?

"A few years. After I left the priesthood, I went a bit wild exploring my sexuality."

I jerk away and spin around to face him. "Wait. What? You're a priest?"

"Not anymore." He frowns. "Is that a problem?"

I put my hands over my face and back away. He's not only going to be freaked out if he finds out what I am. He's going to hate me. He might send me to hell. Can he do that? Do priests carry holy water and crosses in their pockets? Does holy water stay holy after they quit?

"Brin."

I peek at him through my fingers.

"What's wrong? Have you had a bad experience with religion or something?"

"Or something. Why did you leave?"

"I realised I was attracted to men as much as women. At first, I tried to ignore my desire for men. It wasn't as if I could act on it. I'd taken a vow of celibacy. But I soon realised it wasn't going to go away, and I became increasingly uncomfortable serving a church whose doctrine told me those desires were wrong."

I lower my hands while he's speaking, letting them hang loose at my sides. "That can't have been easy."

"It wasn't. Choosing to leave not just the priesthood but the church as well was one of the hardest decisions I've ever had to make. I wrestled with it for a long time, but eventually, I knew it was what I had to do."

"And then you trained to become a nurse?"

"Yes."

"You wanted to care for people?"

"And to continue to serve the community in any way I could."

"What's the Catholic Church's view on Daddy kink?"

He laughs. "They'd frown upon it. I'm a very sinful man these days. Bisexual. Into kink. Having sex with a beautiful younger man while his great-aunt is asleep upstairs."

"You make a habit of that, do you?"

"No." He steps closer.

I move backwards, maintaining the gap between us. "Did you know how to do exorcisms when you were a priest?"

"No. Where did that question come from?"

I shrug, hoping to appear nonchalant. "I've seen plenty of films with them in. You think the house is haunted. Maybe you'd want to do an exorcism."

"I can't do them."

Good news for me. "You've already committed enough sins with me. You probably don't want to add any more to the list."

Ian presses his lips together. "Is my past that much of a turn-off for you?"

I hug myself. "No. Not exactly."

"Then what is it? I'm getting whiplash from the way you keep blowing hot and cold. I used to be a priest. I'm not anymore. I couldn't maintain faith in a God who would deny me simply because of who I choose to love. I don't view what we did or might do as a sin. I want you, Brin." He moves closer as he talks. Close enough to gently grasp my shoulders.

"For sex?"

He sighs. "If that's all that's on offer, yes."

"You shouldn't want me, Ian."

"Why?"

"Because—" Shut up. Shut up.

He crooks his finger under my chin and tilts my face, forcing me to meet his stare or close my eyes. I choose the former, which is a mistake. My insides tremble. My body aches. I want him so badly.

"Because other men have abandoned you?"

"I wanted them to."

"Why? Don't you think you deserve more than sex?"

My chin trembles. "Because—" Shut up.

He bends down, bringing his mouth close to mine. "Tell me, boy."

My knees go weak. "I can't, Daddy." My throat is thick with emotion.

"You can tell me anything."

"You'll hate me. You'll— You'll be scared of me."

He raises his eyebrows and widens his eyes. "Scared of you? Why? I can't imagine ever being scared of you."

"You don't know me." I pull away and put distance between us. "Do you want to know who I am?"

"Yes."

"Do you want to know what I am?"

His brow crumples. "I don't understand."

"You will." I lift my chin, meet his questioning gaze, and allow my true form to reassert itself.

I fall on my arse. I can't breathe as a vice made of fear tightens around my chest.

Brin has changed. His eyes are no longer dark brown but blood red and glowing like the embers of a dying fire. Two horns have sprouted from his head, short, black, and twisting. The ridges gleam red in the pale late-autumn sunlight. His ears have elongated to a sharp point. A large pair of wings unfurls from his back, black and bat-like. A tail swishes behind him, long, black, slender, and flexible as a cat's, with a tuft of hair at the end, like the tip of a lion's tail. Apart from his eyes, his face is unchanged, and his skin is the same tawny shade. Warmth radiates off him, overpowering the chill in the air. I can't take my eyes off him. Can't move, let alone stand and run. Not that I want to. I want to bask in his terrible beauty.

"This is what I am." His voice, though trembling, is the same as it was. "This is why I can't have the nice things you want to give. Why I'm happy for men to have me and then leave without a second glance."

"You're— You're a—" It's hard to speak, but as I become accustomed to his appearance, the vice around my chest loosens.

"A demon," he says in a matter-of-fact tone.

"A—?" My mind can't wrap itself around what I see.

He crouches, hugging his knees with his arms and tail. "Demon."

Demons are in the bible, of course. But even when my faith was at its strongest, I believed them to be allegories rather than reality.

"Do you still want to do all the things you talked about?" he whispers. "Fuck me? Embrace me? Fall asleep beside me? Wake up holding me? Spank me for being naughty? Call me boy? Have me call you Daddy? Could you do all those things to this?" He gestures to himself.

Could I? I wipe my hand over my face. My thoughts are spinning in circles. Brin is a demon. He has horns. Wings. A tail. He's not human.

Everything I was ever taught about demons comes crashing into my head. Led by Lucifer, they were angels who defied the will of God and were cast out of heaven. The church believes it is in a demon's core nature to tempt humans into sin and convince them to abandon their faith in God. It's their mission. Demons are capable of taking on any form. In Corinthians, it's mentioned that Lucifer can make himself look like an angel of light. Despite that, they're almost exclusively drawn as vile, hideous creatures, no doubt to conjure fear in people.

Brin is neither hideous nor disguising himself as an angel. His vulnerability is proof enough that he has revealed his true self to me, which must have taken great courage. Yet here I am, on my arse, barely able to speak, let alone offer him any comfort and reassurance like a good Daddy should.

"I didn't think so." He stands and turns on his heel, the movement of his wings creating a warm breeze that ruffles my hair.

Does he think I'm horrified? Repulsed? Scared?

"Brin."

He keeps walking, hands clenched.

I can't let him leave, not like this. I scramble to my feet and stumble after him. His wings are too large for me to be able to hold him from behind, so I manoeuvre in front of him.

He stops, his stare defiant yet full of resignation.

"You're—"

"A demon," he snaps. "We've covered that already."

"I was going to say beautiful. You're beautiful."

He sneers. "If you're afraid I'm going to do something awful to you if you piss me off, don't be. As Mother says, I'm too gentle for my own good."

"Mother?"

"Martha."

"Martha is—?" My brain might explode if it has to take in much more.

"My mother."

How is that possible? I clutch my hair and take a few deep breaths. Am I dreaming? Have I fallen and hit my head? I push my coat and jumper sleeve back and pinch my forearm. It smarts.

"What did you do that for?" Brin asks.

"I wasn't sure any of this is real."

"How is hurting yourself meant to prove it is?"

A smile creeps up on me. "Never mind. This is real. You are a demon." Saying it out loud is oddly calming. My heartbeat has almost slowed to its normal pace. The vice around my chest is all but gone. "You're a demon."

"Yes." He folds his arms and pouts. "Can you get to the running away screaming part, please?"

I jerk my head back. "What?"

"That's what happened the one time I couldn't hold my human form during sex. He saw my eyes and ran screaming."

My heart breaks. "I'm not going to run screaming."

Brin tilts his head to one side. "What are you going to do?"

Good question. What am I going to do? My emotions are a jumbled mess. I have questions, urges, and desires, many of which conflict with one another.

"It's hard for you to look human?" I ask.

"It takes a lot of concentration. Funnily enough, concentrating during sex isn't as easy as it sounds. My eyes tend to change first. I don't know why."

Which is why he was so insistent on turning away from me yesterday instead of frotting face to face.

"You've never shown your true self to anyone before?"

"Other than Mother, no."

"Why me?"

He shrugs. "I wanted more than once with you, probably because of that Daddy-boy stuff. It resonates." He presses his hand to his chest. "Plus, you're gorgeous." He scuffs his boot over the grass. "But more than anything, I want to be able to be my true self with a man. It's stupid of me to want that. I can't have it. No one would want me like this. You won't want me like this."

"Won't I?" I step so close we're sharing body heat. Or rather, I'm sharing his. He has a field of warmth around him that could defy even the coldest winter day.

"How could you? You were terrified when I first revealed myself."

"I admit, falling on my arse wasn't my finest moment. And yes, I was scared. And shocked. It's not every day a stunning young man turns into a demon in front of me."

Brin chuckles. "I guess not. So, where do we go from here? What happens next?"

"This." I cup his face and kiss him gently, surprising myself.

Brin blinks repeatedly as I release him. He touches his lips, his eyes wide. "You're not freaking out anymore?"

"Oh, I am. Big time. But you're still the most beautiful thing I've ever seen and the most vibrant person—demon—I've ever met."

"I bet I'm the only demon you've ever met."

"That I know of. Most importantly, Brin, you're still you."

"Is that good?"

"Yes. It's very, very good."

Brin dips his chin as his cheeks flush with colour. Demons can blush. Interesting.

"Thank you."

He frowns. "What for?"

"Having the courage to show me the real you. It can't have been easy."

"I had to, for all the reasons I mentioned earlier."

"You want me to want the real you."

"Yes." He chuckles. "By the way, that age gap you were worried about? Flip it. I told you I'm not as young as I look. I meant it."

My jaw drops. "How old are you?"

"Sixty. Maybe. I lose track. Years don't mean much to me except watching Mother grow older." Sadness strangles his voice, making me want to hold and comfort him.

"Martha is human?"

"Yes."

"Why do you look twentysomething?"

"I don't age as you do. I did, to start with. I was a baby, a toddler, a child. But after twenty or so years, I stopped ageing. I'll never appear to be any older than I am now."

I can't imagine what it's like for him, having to watch his mother grow older while he remains static.

"The house isn't haunted by anything other than me." His voice has a forced lightness to it. I can understand his need to change the subject.

"You're a ghost too?"

"No, just a demon who can turn into flames."

The fire. Of course. I resist the urge to slap my hand against my forehead. "You warmed the tea."

He laughs. "Seriously? That's what's on your mind right now?" He steps back and bows elaborately. "Brin, demonic tea warmer, at your service."

"You don't visit Martha, do you? You live here."

"Yes. Another necessary lie, sorry. Nethermire is my home, my sanctuary, and my prison."

"Your prison?"

"I can't leave. It's for my own safety. Mother has put wards around the perimeter of the grounds. Demons can't cross it. So none can get in, but by the same token, I can't get out."

"Why?"

"My father broke the laws of hell by having a child with a human. They came for us when I was a baby. Father drew them away while Mother put the wards up."

Martha's choice of words makes sense now. Imprisoned rather than in prison. Mal truly is out of her reach.

Brin drops to his knees. "I'm sorry for all the lies, Ian. But I can't tell anyone and everyone what I am."

I kneel and gently grasp his shoulders. "Of course not. I understand. Are the wards on the house and grounds permanent?"

"No. Mother has to renew them every few days."

My heart lurches into my throat. Martha is old. She's fit and healthy now, but she won't be forever. What will happen when she's too infirm to renew the wards? What will happen when she passes? The thought of Brin being alone, at the mercy of whatever forces want him, sickens me.

"A priest fucking a demon must be a special kind of sin. I'm sorry. If I'd known—"

I press my fingers to his lips. "Ex-priest. And you didn't know. And if it is a sin, I'll gladly commit it again." I kiss him. "And again."

"Daddy."

I shiver with desire. The word holds limitless power over me, especially coming from his lips.

"Will you be my Daddy?" Hope sparkles in his blood-red eyes. Vulnerability tugs his lips down.

"Is that what you want?"

"Yes. I want you to take care of me. You said that's what a Daddy does."

"It is."

"I've always been a boy without realising it. I did ask you to teach me how not to be naughty the first time we met."

I laugh. "You did. Although I quite like it when you're naughty and bratty."

"That's useful, considering it's my natural state." He puts his hand on my chest. "Will you?"

"Be your Daddy?"

He nods.

A demon is asking me to be his Daddy. Could this day get any stranger? My world has been tipped upside down and turned inside out. Demons are real. Does that mean angels are too? Did the war in heaven happen? Are demons truly fallen angels? I could well believe it as I stare into Brin's questioning eyes and stroke his black hair behind his ear. I doubt I'll ever get the answers I seek, but what I do know is that his revelation hasn't muted my desire for him. If anything, it's stronger than before. Brin was a stunning human, but his true form is beautiful beyond words.

"Yes. I will be your Daddy." The words slip from my lips freely and easily. Warmth settles in my chest. I mean them. I want to be Brin's Daddy. I want everything that comes with that title and responsibility. "Will you be my boy?"

"Yes, Daddy."

I wrap him in my arms, one across his shoulders, the other around his lower back, beneath his wings—how his T-shirt wasn't ripped to tatters, I'll never know—and kiss him fiercely. His body warms mine, making me want to take my coat off. Probably my jumper too. Fuck it.

I want us to be naked. Want to press my body against his, want to be intertwined in his willowy limbs. Want to touch and taste him. Want to lose myself in him completely. If wanting him is a sin, I'll gladly accept the stain on my soul.

I cling to Ian and press my face against his shoulder. The earnest cadence of his voice should have been enough to convince me he truly wants me. The fact he's here, holding me, rather than halfway home should be convincing too. But doubts flicker inside me. Is all he said nothing but hollow words? Is he hiding his fear until he's able to leave? Will he return with someone from the church who can perform an exorcism? Would that work?

He rubs my shoulders above my wings. "Talk to me, boy." It's a command. I feel it in my bones, along with the urge to obey.

"Do you want to be naughty with me?"

He chuckles. "What are you thinking?"

I lift my head. "Fuck me."

"Here? Now?"

"Yes, Daddy."

Is it wrong of me to need to know if he truly wants to? He can say it a million times over, but I need him to show me the truth of his words through actions. And if he can't, I'd rather know that now.

I tug at his jumper. "I can keep you warm."

"I know, but—" He glances around.

"No one can see us, Daddy."

We have no neighbours, the walls surrounding the garden are tall, and the trees are taller. We're not even close to being in direct line of sight of the house, and I know Mother isn't going to come looking for us. She sent me out here to find Ian.

"But if you don't want to, that's okay. We could talk some more instead before you have to go home. I'm sure you have lots to do."

Ian pinches his brows together. "You're giving me an out."

"I am." I pull away from his embrace and stand. "It's okay if you've changed your mind or didn't mean what you said. If that's the case, you can and should go. I'll only ask one thing of you. Don't tell anyone about me."

"Brin." Ian stands and grasps my shoulders. "I meant every word. I want you. I want to be your Daddy."

Does he? Truly? "I'm sorry for doubting you, Daddy."

He moves his hands to my waist. "You want to be naughty, boy?"

"Yes, Daddy."

"Out here in the garden?"

"Yes, Daddy."

He slides his right hand to my lower back and slips his fingers into my jeans. "You're not wearing underwear. Again. Naughty boy."

"I don't own any."

He chuckles. "Why doesn't that surprise me?" He moves his hand down, grazing the base of my tail. He widens his eyes. "Tail. I almost forgot. I'm sorry. I've got to ask. How are your clothes still intact?"

"Crazy demon magic. My clothes don't turn to ash when I turn into flames and back again either."

"Magic is real?"

"Seriously? The only reason you're not teasing a demon's arsehole right now is because my tail got in the way, and you're going to question whether or not magic is real? Want me to turn into flames to prove it?"

"No." He dips his lips to mine. "It's quite all right. I believe you."

He kisses me softly while he manoeuvres his hand around my tail to stroke my arsehole. "Now I am teasing a demon's arse."

"It feels so good, Daddy."

"Damn." Ian leans his forehead against mine.

"What?"

"No lube or condoms. This was an apology visit. I wasn't even sure you'd be here. I certainly wasn't trying to get into your pants."

"I don't wear pants."

He snorts. "Into your jeans, then."

"But, Daddy, I want you to try to get into my jeans."

"I noticed."

I lift my chin and peck his lips. "We don't need condoms. I'm a demon. I can't catch anything humans can pass on."

"You're sure?"

"Positive. I'm not lying."

He cups my cheek. "I don't think you are."

"I wouldn't blame you if you did. I did lie to you for weeks."

"That's behind us now. No lies from now on. Only the truth."

"I promise, Daddy."

"So do I, boy." He kisses me. "We still need lube."

"Do we? Spit and pre-cum would work just as well."

Ian pulls a face.

I laugh. "All right, almost as well. Well, enough. I want to feel your cock inside me, Daddy, right now. I don't want to go back to the house to find lube."

"I don't want to hurt you."

"Says the man who wants to spank my arse if I'm naughty."

"It's different."

"Oh, to self-lubricate." I pout. "Please, Daddy. If it's too much, I'll tell you, and then we can go to the house to find lube."

He sighs. "All right, but you have to tell me if it's painful."

"I will. How do you want me, Daddy?"

"Aside from naked?"

I giggle. "Naked is a given. I want you naked too, Daddy."

He purses his lips as he skims his stare over me. Is he debating the logistics of sex now I have wings and a tail?

"You could bend me over the bench. If you stand tall, my wings shouldn't get in the way."

"Or I could sit or lie on the bench, and you could ride my cock."

"Oh! I love that idea, Daddy."

"But bending you over the bench while I warm up your arse is a good idea. How will I take your clothes off?"

"It'll be easier than you think, promise."

I grasp the hem of his jumper, tug it over his head, and drop it onto the bench. I can keep him warm, but stone still won't be comfortable. Our clothes will give him a little bit of padding. I take his T-shirt off next before undoing his blue jeans. I drop to my knees as I pull them down his legs. He kicks off his shoes and then, with my help, steps out of his jeans. I remove his underpants next but leave his socks. They'll protect his feet from any stray pebbles that might be hiding in the long grass.

I rock onto my heels and gaze at him. "You're beautiful, Daddy. Can I suck your cock? I'm good at it."

He groans. "I don't doubt it, boy. But no, not yet."

I pout and whine. "But I want to make you come."

"Oh, I will, when my cock is buried inside your arse."

I shiver. "We could do both?"

He puts his hands on his hips. "I wish. But I'll need time to recover. Usually, at least thirty minutes, sometimes longer, if the orgasm is mind-blowing."

"Do you want to learn another fun fact about demons?"

Ian holds his hand out. "You're going to tell me you don't need to rest between orgasms, aren't you?"

I hold his hand and let him pull me to my feet. "Yup. And we never dry orgasm either. Having watched plenty of human porn, I can tell you we produce a lot more cum than humans too."

"Are you trying to make me jealous?"

"No. Just letting you know how much fun you could have with me." I press myself against him and stroke his chest. "I love your chest fur." I rub my face in it and lick one nipple and then the other.

He shivers and groans as his nipples harden into nubs. "You have too many clothes on, boy." Doubt fills his eyes as he grasps the hem of my T-shirt. "I'm going to wreck it."

"If you do, you do. I have plenty more." I kick my boots off and then lift my arms. "Undress me, Daddy."

He taps the end of my nose. "I'm the one who's supposed to give the orders, naughty boy."

"Please undress me, Daddy?"

"Better."

He lifts my T-shirt. As he predicted, it rips on my wings, leaving it a sorry cotton rag. It gets added to Ian's clothes on the bench, the seat of which is now mostly covered. Taking my jeans off is easier. My tail is thin and supple enough to slip through a small hole in the seam.

Ian steps back. I nip my lower lip between my teeth as his lusty stare slowly travels over my body from head to toe and back up.

"You are the most stunning creature I have ever seen."

"Thank you, Daddy."

"Now be a good boy and lean over the back of the bench."

I move behind the bench and bend over, with my stomach resting on the back and my hands pressed against the clothing-covered seat. As Ian comes to stand behind me, I flick my tail up and out of the way, giving him easy access to my arse, and fold my wings tight against my back. Excitement ripples through me. Surely, he wouldn't have got naked with me if he wasn't going to fuck me? For the first time, I'm going to experience the touch of man while in my true form. I almost come on the spot.

"Lots of cum, huh?" he asks.

"So much cum."

"And multiple orgasms without needing to rest?"

"Uh-huh."

He brushes his lips over my ear. "I'm going to put that to the test, boy."

He rubs his cock against my arse, reaches around me, and gives my dick a good, hard tug. I whimper as pre-cum leaks from the tip. He gathers it on his fingers to make my cock slick.

"I'm going to make you come, and then I'm going to use your cum to lubricate your arse."

My knees weaken. My arms shake. "Oh, Daddy."

He holds my hip with his free hand and ruts against me as he jacks me off. He rubs his hand up and down my length quickly. This is a sexy starter. I'm happy for it to be quick and frantic.

"That feels amazing, Daddy."

"I'm glad, boy. I want to make you come. I want you to jizz all over my hand."

"I will, Daddy. I will."

I gasp and groan as he squeezes my cock a little harder. It doesn't take long for my balls to get heavy and draw up tight. I embrace my orgasm with a throaty moan. He moves his hand to cover the head of my cock. My body shudders as my cock jerks in his hand, and my balls empty into his cupped hand.

"So much cum," he croons, lifting his hand to show me. It's thick, white, and dripping free of his palm.

"You'd better use it quick, Daddy, before it ends up watering the grass."

He laughs as he smears it over my arse crack. "It's so hot."

"Demon," I say in a sing-song tone.

"You are very hot."

"So hot I'm on fire." I glance over my shoulder and wink.

"I'd rather you didn't turn to fire while I've got my fingers up your arse. Or my cock, for that matter."

"Don't worry, Daddy, I won't." I groan as he presses his finger against my hole. "I need you, Daddy."

He pushes his finger and my cum deep inside me. "Damn, your arse is like a furnace."

"Too hot?" Is he going to stop? Is he going to change his mind?

"No, boy. It's perfect. It will help you warm up faster." He thrusts his finger, quickly adding a second to stretch me more.

"I'm having a hard time imagining you taking a vow of celibacy."

"I assure you I did, and I took it seriously. I didn't break it. But when I left the priesthood, I went out and had a lot of fun."

I snigger. "I can imagine you making up for however many years of abstinence." I arch my back so he can get his fingers deeper.

He slides a third inside me. My cum creates a wet sound as he draws his fingers back and forth.

"I'm ready, Daddy. I'm ready for your cock."

"Patience, boy."

"Patience is not one of my virtues, Daddy. I need you inside me now." I stamp my foot.

"I am inside you."

"Your cock!"

"I'm enjoying playing with your arse. Enjoying taking my time and hearing you whimper."

"I'll whimper more with your cock inside me. And you'll have more fun with your cock inside me too. Please, Daddy. Please. Fuck me. Fuck me now."

"You are so impatient and such a brat." He moves his hand from my hip and squeezes my arse cheek. "Maybe you need to be reminded who's in charge?"

"You are, Daddy." I wriggle on his fingers. "But I still want you to fuck me right now."

"Or I could make you come like this. And then come again with me inside you."

"You'll have to work harder to make me come with your fingers alone."

"Is that a challenge, boy?"

I purse my lips and then lift my chin. "Yes, Daddy."

"Challenge accepted."

He adds a fourth finger and uses them to fuck me hard, driving deep, pulling out so only the very tips of them are still inside me before pushing back in again. Every fast, deep thrust is accompanied by a slight sting. Maybe lube would have been better than cum, but I'm beyond caring about a smidgen of pain. His cock is bigger than four fingers. Then again, if he has his way, I'll have produced more cum before I enjoy his cock, and he is going to get his way.

"Daddy, I—"

He cups his free hand over the head of my cock, collecting my hot, sticky cum as my body shudders and shivers. I tremble. My legs and arms shake.

"Daddy."

He pulls his fingers free of me, dips them into the cum he's collected, and then pushes them back inside. After a few delicious thrusts, he removes them again and then walks to the other side of the bench and makes himself comfortable on it. He half sits, half lies, with his back propped against the arm of the bench. He uses the rest of my cum to slick his cock up. Fuck, it's long, fat, veiny, and delicious enough to devour with my arse or my mouth.

"Come sit on my cock, boy. Ride me."

"You... really want me to?"

He frowns, and sadness fills his eyes. "Still doubting me, boy?"

"I'm sorry. I-I don't want you to do anything you'll regret. You can't take this back, Daddy."

"I won't want to. I want to fuck you. Unless you've changed your mind?"

"No. I want you, Daddy. I need you."

"Then come here, boy, and ride my cock."

"Yes, Daddy."

My legs are unsteady as I make my way around the bench. I straddle him, kneeling tall above his cock. He holds it steady for me while I sink onto it. I arch my spine and tip my head back. There's a slight burn, but no more than with his fingers, probably thanks to the second round of cum he enticed out of me.

Once he's fully seated inside me, and his balls are nestled against my arse, I lean forwards and stare into his eyes. He holds my hips and thrusts his upwards, slowly and gently at first. I move my palms in circles over his nipples and stroke my tail down the insides of his thighs.

"Oh, Brin. I won't last long. You're so hot and tight. I've never experienced anything like this."

I laugh. "Once you fuck a demon, you'll never want to go back."

"You're right."

I lick my lips. "I was joking."

"I'm not."

I whimper.

He thrusts harder and deeper, but not faster. "Tell me if it hurts."

"It doesn't, Daddy. You did a good job of warming me up. You're taking good care of me."

He grunts and fucks me with more vigour. He uses his grip on me to help me rise and fall at the perfect pace, so I'm taking his cock as deep as it will go. The prominent veins on his length provide extra stimulation, and it isn't long before the pressure in my groin is too intense to bear.

"Daddy!" I fling my head back and unfurl my wings as I come. My cum spurts over him, splattering his chest, chin, beard, and lips.

He grunts and groans, his thrusts frantic for the few seconds it takes him to orgasm inside me. His cum floods me, cooling my channel. He stares into my eyes as he licks my cum off his lips. It's enough to make me orgasm again, less violently than before.

"You weren't kidding when you said you didn't need a rest period, were you, boy?"

I grin. "Want to make me come again, Daddy?"

He chuckles and shakes his head. "I don't have the energy." He holds his arms out. "Come here."

I bite my tongue so as not to comment on his unintentional pun and lie on his chest. His cock is still inside me. He can keep it inside me all day if he wants. My hot cum squishes between us, but I don't care, and he doesn't seem to either.

He wraps his arms around me and kisses my forehead. "That was amazing, boy. Now do you believe I want you?"

"Yes, Daddy. I believe."

Although Brin is keeping me warm, my back, shoulders, and hips are getting stiff and sore from lying on the stone bench. Not that it's enough to compel me to move. I'm still half expecting to wake up and discover this was all some strange erotic dream, while the other half of me would rather stay in this fantasy forever.

I move my hand to stroke Brin's hair but catch one of his horns instead. It's smooth, warm, and hard. I run my fingertips up the curling length, bumping over the ridges. Brin looks up, eyelids heavy as he smiles.

I snatch my hand away. "Sorry."

"What for? It was nice."

"Nice?"

He nods. "Mother used to stroke my horns when I was little and couldn't sleep. It's comforting when she does it." His red eyes gleam mischievously. "I bet you could make horn stroking sexy."

"You've got sex on the brain, naughty boy."

"Yes, I do." He wriggles, stimulating my flaccid cock inside him. "Can you blame me?"

I chuckle. "I suppose not. Do you want me to pull out?"

He pouts. "Don't you dare, Daddy. I'm enjoying being your cock warmer."

Emphasis on the warmer. All arses are warm, but his is next level. "If you want to be my boy—my submissive—we need some safewords."

Do demons need safewords? Will he have the same limits as a human?

"Um, why?"

"In case you need me to stop or slow down. For example, if I spank you for being naughty, you might not like it. Or you might enjoy it but only up to a point. Safewords are a clear way to communicate when things don't feel right."

"Couldn't I just tell you?"

"Sometimes, in kink, no doesn't mean no."

"Huh?"

"It might be part of a role-playing scene for the submissive to say no or stop and have their Dom carry on anyway. It would have been discussed beforehand, which is one of the reasons safewords are used. They're words you wouldn't use for any other reason during a scene, so the meaning is never ambiguous."

"Hm, humans are strange, but it makes sense, I suppose. I don't think I'd be interested in pretending I don't want sex."

I laugh. "I didn't think you would be. It was the first example that popped into my head."

"Phew." He strokes my chest hair. "I've spent a long time having to pretend I'm something I'm not during sex. I don't want to do that with you."

"You don't have to. I promise."

Brin twirls his finger around my nipple. "What is this?"

"My nipple?"

He laughs. "No. This thing between us? Sex? A fling? An affair?"

"Neither of us is dating anyone else, so it can't be an affair."

"True."

I sigh. "I don't know what this is. Sex? Yes. A fling? Yes. Could it be more? Only time will tell."

"More." Brin's voice is wistful. "Let's not get ahead of ourselves." He kisses my chest. "For now, I'd like to enjoy sex and getting to stroke this amazing carpet of hair whenever I want." He pulls a face like he's sucking a sour sweet. "Well, whenever you come to visit, which isn't quite the same thing. If I had my way, I'd keep you in my dungeon as my Daddy slave."

"You... have a dungeon?"

He sniggers. "No, but it was worth saying it for the look on your face. Don't panic, Daddy. I have no intention of trapping you here. I couldn't even if I wanted to, which I don't. I want you to want me of your own free will."

"I do." I stroke his horn.

He smiles so wide his eyes turn into half moons. "It's amazing to hear you say that. It makes me feel warm and fuzzy here." He touches his chest. "Or maybe it's your chest hair making me feel fuzzy." He winks.

"You might have an obsession."

"With you?"

"My chest hair."

"Yes, yes, I do." He presses his face against my chest and then rubs it from side to side. "I have a thing for furry Daddies now. Especially ones with big cocks." He tightens his arse muscles around my length.

I gasp. Why can't I have a faster recovery period? "Sorry, boy, I'm not ready for another round."

"That's okay. Your cock feels nice inside me, hard or soft. I could stay here for the rest of the day." He rests his cheek on my chest and closes his eyes. "We should probably go inside soon."

"Will Martha be worrying?"

"I doubt it. She sent me out to talk to you."

"Then we can stay here for as long as you want."

"Not much longer. I have a cuddly Daddy beneath me, but you're lying on stone, and that can't be comfortable."

"It's not."

"Then we should get up." He doesn't. "I could give you a tour of the house, ending in my bedroom."

"I'd like that."

He moves a few minutes later, thrusting onto my cock twice before pulling off me and standing. His chest and abdomen are streaked with drying cum. I'm covered in it too. Cum dribbles down his inner thighs, a combination of his and mine.

"I've got nothing to clean you up with," I say.

He tugs his T-shirt from beneath me and uses it to brush me down and then himself.

"It should be me doing that, boy."

"Why?"

"It's my job to take care of you."

"Oh, because you're the Daddy?"

"Yes."

"Noted. I'll let you do it next time."

I stand and get dressed. Thankfully, my clothes are mostly clean. Brin puts his jeans and boots on, but his T-shirt is too ripped, not to mention cum stained, to wear. I hold Brin's hand as we amble through the garden, neither of us in a hurry to return to the house.

"We never did choose safewords, boy." I make a mental note to keep serious conversations on track from now on. Brin is a very distracting boy.

"You've used them before. What would you suggest?"

"Do you know what traffic lights are?"

Brin wrinkles his nose. "I might not have been outside Nethermire, but I watch stuff. I know stuff, including what traffic lights are."

I squeeze his hand. "Sorry."

"It's okay. I admit my view of the world might be somewhat skewed. It's entirely formed by what Mother has told me and by watching TV and films. The internet has been the biggest help, though. People put some crazy stuff on there."

It's going to take time to get used to the fact that Brin is older than me. He doesn't seem older at all. He's too vibrant and wide-eyed. He doesn't have any of the cynicism that usually comes with age. Is that because he's led such a sheltered life?

What were we talking about? Right. Safewords. Don't let Brin derail the conversation.

"Traffic lights make good safewords," I say.

"I don't get it."

"Red means stop."

"Oh! And green means go. I get it now."

"And yellow?"

"Um, slow down?"

I smile. "Yes."

"But I only need to use them if I need them?"

"They're a safety net. If you use them, I will listen."

"Red."

I stop.

Brin sniggers. "Just testing you. Green."

I roll my eyes as we walk. "They're to use when we're doing kinky things, not to control me on a whim, naughty boy."

He pouts. "Aw, but that would be so much fun."

"No."

"Sorry, Daddy. I'll be good and only use them if I really, truly need them. Not to stop-start you during sex, as fun as that would be."

I chuckle and shake my head. "Safewords are serious, boy."

"Of course. I can be serious."

I lean down and kiss his temple. "You are chaotic."

"You've just noticed?"

"No. It's one of the things that makes you so irresistible."

"Aw! That's the nicest thing anyone has ever said to me."

I stop and tug him to me so our chests are touching. "You are incredible, Brin, and don't let anyone tell you otherwise."

His smile quivers into a fragile line. "Thank you, Daddy." He pushes up onto his toes and kisses me, a soft, lingering kiss which melts my heart.

Martha is on her way up the stairs as we come through the front door. She hangs onto the banister to steady herself as she turns.

She smiles as she looks between us. "Good talk?"

My cheeks flush with heat.

Brin holds his head high. "The best. Thank you for shoving me out the door, Mother."

"He knows everything?"

"Yes. Now I don't have to remember to call you Martha anymore."

"I was on my way for a nap, but if you have any questions, I'd be happy to answer them another time, Ian."

"Thank you."

"You young men might want to shower." Chuckling, she goes upstairs, her walking stick thudding against the wood, which squeaks underfoot.

I puff my cheeks out. "She knows we had sex."

Brin gestures to his stomach and chest with the cum stained T-shirt. "It's obvious."

"Yup. I feel like a teenager."

"There's no need to be embarrassed. Mother and Father were lovers for decades."

I frown. "Decades? How can that be?"

"It's time to take you on a tour of the house."

He takes my hand and leads me through the ground floor. There are two more reception rooms, aside from the two I've already seen. One has a huge TV, three different game consoles, and a treasure trove of DVDs and games, along with a comfy sofa. The other is a hobby room, with dozens of unfinished projects in different types of crafts from painting and sculpture to engraving, crochet, clothes making, and woodwork.

The sunroom has a mishmash of furniture from different decades. Potted plants cover every surface. Despite it being autumn outside, the sunroom is warm, and many of the flowers are in bloom, giving the room a fragrant scent.

"Mother loves gardening," Brin says proudly.

We go upstairs next. The first floor is divided into six bedrooms and a master bathroom. He shows me all but Martha's room and his. Every fireplace has wood ready for a fire in it. The top floor, in the eaves of the house, has four bedrooms, all much smaller than their counterparts downstairs. I imagine that, at one point, they were servants' quarters.

The final room Brin takes me into is full of paintings and photographs, all sepia or black and white. None are modern, let alone in colour. They're all of the same woman. The one who was in the portrait in the front room. Martha's grandmother. Only judging by the clothing in some of the paintings, they predate the Victorian era, which is impossible. Isn't it?

"They're all of Mother," Brin says, confirming my suspicion. "Father loved painting her. He was very excited when the camera was first invented."

"How old is Martha?"

"I don't know exactly. She could tell you."

"You said she was human."

"She is. Something about being with Father stopped her ageing. She was in her early twenties for a long time, but when he was taken away, she started getting old again." He shoves his hands into his pockets. "She won't tell me what he did to stop her getting old, only that I can't do whatever it was. Not for her anyway."

I move in front of him so I can embrace him.

"I'm all right, Daddy, but I appreciate the hug." He briefly rests his head against my shoulder before pulling away and smiling brightly.

"You've seen the house. You've explored me quite thoroughly. What would you like to do now?"

"Having a shower might not be a bad idea. I have more questions, if you don't mind?"

"Not at all, but let's go to my room and have that shower." He pinches his bottom lip between his teeth and waggles his eyebrows. "Maybe after some fun? You must have recovered by now. I have lube in my room."

Warmth presses against my groin. My cock twitches in my underpants. "You were sent to tempt me, weren't you, naughty boy?"

"Into having lots of sex? Yes, Daddy. Are you complaining?"

"Not at all. I'd love to see your room."

"And explore me some more?"

"Yes. I'd like that a lot."

"Y ou had questions?" I say as I lie in bed with Ian.

We're naked, filthy, having not worked up the energy to shower yet, and he's stroking my back between my wings in the most delightful way. My head rests on his chest, my ear pressed over his heart, which beats slowly. He seems relaxed, content even. He's certainly not acting like a man who's trying to fool me into believing he's into me until he can make his escape. I shouldn't doubt him, but it's hard not to.

"All I know about demons is what the church taught me. Is any of that true?" Ian asks.

"I don't know how much I'll be able to help, but I'll do my best."

"Does Lucifer exist?"

"Oh, so that isn't just a TV series? The actor who plays Lucifer is hot."

Ian chuckles. "No. According to the bible, Lucifer was once one of God's most beloved angels. But he led a war in heaven and was cast out of it."

"Sounds exciting. But I have no clue."

"You know nothing about hell?"

"No. Mother has never talked about it except to tell me that's where Father is imprisoned. I don't know if Father told her about hell and she simply doesn't want to share her knowledge or if he was tight-lipped about it." I twirl my fingertip around his nipple. "I'm afraid I'm not going to be much help if you want to know about demons and hell. I'm probably the worst demon in existence."

"Perhaps, but you make up for it by being the sexiest."

I snort-laugh. "And you're basing that on—what?"

"The images and drawings of demons. They are depicted as ghastly creatures."

"Sounds like bad press to me."

Ian smiles. "You're probably right."

I rake my fingers through his carpet of chest hair. "Do you have any questions I might be able to answer?"

"Do you need to eat?" He pinches his eyes shut. "Forget that. You ate that cake." He hums, and his cock twitches.

"It's a valid question. For all you know, I might need to feast on the souls of humans."

Ian opens his eyes and stares at me. "You're joking, aren't you?"

"Am I?" I lick my way up his chest and peck his lips. "Oo! Maybe I feed on sexual energy. Then I'd need to keep you as my sex slave. Would you like that? Being kept here to be used for sex? I promise I'd feed you."

"You are a brat."

"So you keep saying." I nip his ear lobe. "But you like it."

"I do." His voice is a low rumble, which makes me shiver.

"Yes, I need to eat. Both food and wood. I love cakes and all things sweet."

Ian frowns. "Wood?"

"Yes. I feast on it when I turn to flames."

"Which is why all the fireplaces have logs in them."

"Yes. The chimneys are all interconnected. So once I've turned into flames, I can move from room to room at will and spy on Mother's guests and creep out unsuspecting nurses." I wink.

"Naughty." He taps my nose.

I grin.

"How did you learn to turn into flames?"

"By accident. I was tiny. Five, maybe six years old. I don't remember. It was decades ago. Anyway, I decided to climb the bookcase, which fell."

"On top of you?" Panic rises in Ian's voice.

"Yes. Only I did more damage to it. I turned into flames and set it alight." I wince. "I could have burnt the house down."

"But you didn't."

I shake my head. "Mother was so brave. She calmed me down and then helped me put out the flames. I can control fire, in case that's your next question."

"It was."

"The bookcase and everything on it was ruined, as were the floorboards and a large portion of the room. Afterwards, Mother screwed all the big bits of furniture to the wall. Not that I ever tried to climb a bookcase again. I learnt my lesson. Speaking of lessons, she spent months helping me figure out how to control my ability to turn into flames."

"Did Martha also help you learn how to make yourself look human?"

"Yes. Father had done it, so she knew it was possible. She did it so I could interact with people who visited the house. It's not as if I was able to leave to go to school or anything."

Ian strokes my cheek. "I'm sorry."

"It's fine. I had everything I needed here."

"Except company."

"I have Mother. And the TV. And when the eighties rolled around, I got the internet too. The internet is the best invention ever."

Ian laughs. "It did make the world a smaller place."

"It brought the world to me. I could finally talk and interact with people besides Mother. I used to be even more socially awkward than I am now."

Ian arches an eyebrow.

"It's true." I kiss his chest. "Is there anything else you'd like to know?"

"Lots, but you're probably tired of answering them."

"I'm not. It's all part of my devious plan."

"To keep me here as a sex slave?"

I laugh. "Yes."

"I will have to go home. I have work tomorrow." He slides his hand down my back, twirls it around the base of my tail, and then lazily strokes up and down my crack. "But I'll come and visit you soon. I promise."

I angle my chin down, hiding my face from him. "You don't have to. I'll understand if you don't want to come back."

"Boy." His commanding tone forces me to jerk my head up and meet his gaze. "I told you I want to be your Daddy."

"I know, but—"

He puts his fingers under my chin. "You still don't believe me, do you?"

"I do. But how long for? The rest of today? Longer? I've been promised the earth in exchange for sex. They're just words."

"The rest of today." He loops his arm around my chest and pulls me closer so it's easier for him to kiss me. "And for as long as we both want. I'll admit my mind is still reeling, but I cannot deny my attraction to you. I need you. I've never felt such a strong pull to anyone before. Is it sexual desire? Probably. Could it grow into more? Maybe. All I know is I want you, and I can't stand the thought of you turning to a hook-up app and inviting another man into your bed."

"Oo, possessive. That's hot."

"I want to be the one to turn you on and make you come. I want to be the one to protect and take care of you. I want to be your Daddy."

I tremble. "You're so sexy when you talk like that, Daddy."

He puts his hand on my nape and pulls me to him for a long, deep kiss. My toes curl, and my cock twitches.

"So yes, I'm going to go home later. But I will come back. And when I do, I'll show you how much I want you."

"I'm looking forward to it already."

He strokes me between my wings again as he stares at them thoughtfully. "Can you fly?"

"Yes, or at least, I could when I was a child. I haven't stretched my wings since I was younger. It's not as if I can go anywhere."

"Because of the wards."

"Flying around the garden and in and out of the attic loses appeal after a while."

Sadness clouds Ian's eyes. "You've never left Nethermire, not even once?"

I shake my head. "I was born here. I was a few days old when the demons came for me and Father."

"D-do you know what they did to your father?"

"No. Mother says he was imprisoned, but she doesn't know for sure. It's what she wants to believe. What she needs to believe. She doesn't want to imagine that he might be—you know."

Ian holds me tight. "Yes."

We lie still for a while, Ian hugging and stroking me to offer me comfort. Eventually, the sadness from thinking about Father ebbs away.

"There's one thing I'm surprised you haven't asked about," I say.

"What's that?"

"The secret to immortality."

He tips my chin up. "You don't think that's why I want you, do you?"

"No." My voice quivers.

"Boy."

"Maybe. A little. I told you Mother spent decades with Father before I was born, never ageing. I could be like the wotsit from *Indiana Jones*."

"The Holy Grail?"

I click my fingers. "Yes. Oh, wait. That's a God thing. Forget that analogy. Hm, maybe the Philosopher's Stone. It could turn lead into silver or gold and could also be used as an elixir of life."

"It's a myth."

"Eh. Who's to say what is and isn't real? You didn't truly believe in the existence of demons until a couple of hours ago."

"True." He rests his hand on my hip. "You said you didn't know how your father stopped Martha from ageing."

I sigh. "I don't. If I did, I would have kept Mother young if she'd wanted me to. Maybe I can't because I'm half human. I wish—" My chin trembles. "I—"

"I know." Ian hugs me tight again.

I press my face to his furry chest and clench my fists.

"If it helps, Martha is in good health."

"For now."

"Hopefully, for many years to come."

"Yes." I clear my throat. "We should shower."

"Not yet. You need a hug. Let me hold you, boy."

"All right, Daddy."

I cuddle close to him, craving the comfort he's giving me. He's offering me more than I've ever had with a man. I'm surprised by how happy I am to lie in his arms, to be embraced by him, to talk to him, to laugh with him. And I need him to take care of me so, so much. I won't run or hide from him again. Assuming he comes back.

After seeing my last patient, I go to Nethermire House. I need to prove to Brin that everything I said and did yesterday wasn't hollow words and actions. I crave him like a tub of ice cream at the end of a bad day. Martha answers the intercom and opens the gate, but it's Brin who greets me once I've stopped the car in front of the house. He's in his human form, but by the time I've finished showing him how much I need him, his concentration is as wrecked as his arsehole.

We lie in his bed, cuddling, desperately needing to shower. I have a beautiful, chaotic, sensual boy in my arms. Why would I want to move?

"Tell me about your family." Brin combs his fingers through my chest hair.

I've never been with anyone—man or woman—who appreciated my furry chest as much as Brin does.

"What do you want to know?"

"Anything. Everything. Are you close?"

"Yes. I have two brothers. I'm the middle child. We're spread across the country now. Victor, my older brother, is an architect. He co-owns a firm in London. Our parents keep joking that they're going to get him to design a house for them, but it's never happened."

"Why?"

"Financial reasons. Buying land and building a house cost a lot of money. Money they don't have. If I could help them, I would, but neither priests nor nurses earn that much. Besides, they're probably too old to want to bother. Dad is seventy-seven, and Mum is seventy-five."

"A little older than Mother. Well, a little older than she looks, anyway."

"Yes."

"What about your younger brother?"

"Neil is a defence barrister. He settled down in Newcastle with his wife. They have two children. Victor isn't married. To my knowledge, he's never dated. I assume he's asexual, aromantic, or both. We've never discussed it."

"Are your family religious?"

"Nominally. They had the three of us baptised and took us to mass at Christmas and Easter. It wasn't until I was a teenager that I started going more often."

Brin uses the end of his soft tail to stroke my thigh. "What made you decide to become a priest?"

I stare at the ceiling for a long time. The plaster has a few hairline cracks in it. "I felt at home in the church. Whenever I was lost, worried, or afraid, I'd visit a church and find peace there either by talking to a priest or simply by praying. I was drawn to the church. I loved God and wanted to serve him. I also wanted to help and look after people. To offer them guidance and support." I sigh.

"Do you miss it?"

"Sometimes. But as I said before, I couldn't keep serving a god and a church that would call me a sinner for desiring men. It wasn't even as if I had plans to act on my desire. I would have stayed celibate for the rest of my life if the church had accepted me as a bisexual priest. While I wouldn't have been thrown out, I would have been expected to keep my sexuality a secret. Some men can live like that. I couldn't."

"I'm sorry the church wouldn't accept you as you are." Brin purses his lips. "Or maybe I'm not. If they had, I'd never have met you, and my arse wouldn't be full of your cum right now."

"I used to think everything happens for a reason."

Brin wrinkles his nose. "Like fate pulling?"

"I don't believe that our fate is predetermined. I do believe that things are put in front of us to either reward or test us. What we do when we meet those things is entirely up to us."

"Which am I? A reward or a test?"

I laugh. "If you're a test, I failed dismally."

"Or maybe you passed. You're good at making me feel good, Daddy."

"A sex test?"

Brin giggles. "Oo, I like that. You passed, but maybe you can fuck me a few more times to be sure."

"You are wicked."

"And naughty and chaotic. I know. I don't intend to change."

"I wouldn't want you to."

Brin grins. He rubs his face in my chest hair before kissing me between my breast bones and then resting his chin on the same spot. "Were your parents upset when you left the priesthood?"

"Actually, they were more shocked when I told them I wanted to be a priest. It was one of those awkward conversations with long silences where it was clear they didn't know what to say or how to react. They were supportive. My parents have always supported all three of us as much as they could. But I don't think they ever truly understood why I wanted to be a priest. When I told them I was leaving the priesthood and why, they embraced me and told me they loved me."

"That was how you came out to them?"

"Yes." I kiss his hair. "What's your coming out story? You were born in what? The sixties? I appreciate Martha was in love with a demon and that homosexuality was decriminalised in 1967, but you didn't grow up in a very progressive time."

"Nor did you, even though you were probably born twenty or so years after me."

"True. It was illegal for teachers to discuss homosexuality when I was in school. I was surrounded by examples of loving husbands and wives with two-point-four children. That and taking a vow of celibacy is probably why I didn't question my sexuality until I was in my thirties."

"I guess the plus side of being crazy sheltered is that I didn't witness any of that stuff other than through the media. Once I figured out touching my dick was pleasurable as fuck, I realised I was attracted to the men I saw on TV rather than the women. Mother was relieved I was into guys. There was no danger of me getting a man pregnant and moving even farther up hell's hit list. I don't even top."

"Ever?"

"Nah. I tried once but didn't get the same enjoyment out of it. I prefer to be fucked. There's something amazing about having a guy's dick inside me. Especially yours." He groans. "You're so big, and your cock is so veiny. Ugh. I could come just thinking about it. Do you ever bottom?"

"Sometimes."

"You're versatile?"

I shrug. "I prefer to top, but I'm not against bottoming. It's fun as long as I get to stay in charge."

Brin chuckles. "I can't imagine you ever letting someone take charge of you. I can imagine you topping from the bottom. Riding your sub's cock like you own the damn thing. Then again, you would own it, wouldn't you? They'd be your boy."

I raise my eyebrows. "For someone who only discovered kink yesterday, you seem to know a lot about it."

Brin sniggers. "Didn't I tell you the internet is the best invention? It's a treasure trove of information. I might have spent a lot of the day reading. Mother says my mind is like a sponge. I like sucking up knowledge." He waggles his eyebrows. "Knowledge isn't the only thing I like sucking." He brushes the end of his tail over my cock.

I shiver and groan. "We're talking and cuddling, boy."

"Which is fun, but you'd have even more fun if you let me suck your cock. Please, Daddy."

I pull him close and kiss his neck. "Can't you be good for even a few minutes?"

"Thinking about sex and offering to suck your cock is bad?" He widens his eyes and flutters his lashes. The effect is innocent and sexy at the same time, something I didn't think was possible.

"Hm, that was a bad choice of words. Can't you behave for more than a few minutes?"

"Thinking about—"

I put my fingers over his lips. I know exactly what he's going to say. He licks my fingers. I jerk my hand away.

"You like it when I'm naughty, Daddy."

"I do." I stroke his horn. "But I also enjoy holding you."

He rests his cheek on my chest. "Me too. Thank you for coming back."

"I'll come back so often you'll get sick of me."

"Hm, I'm not sure that could happen, but I'm happy for you to try." He tickles his fingers down my ribcage. "I'm sorry for doubting you."

"You've never trusted anyone with your secret before. You put a lot on the line yesterday. You made yourself incredibly vulnerable. I can understand why you would doubt me."

"I'll try not to."

"And I'll keep proving to you that you have no reason to. It's crazy, but thoughts of you consume me."

"That's not a demon thing. At least, I don't think it is. Mother would have told me if I was some kind of sex magnet, right? Then again, those other guys wouldn't have got off and left if I did. Right? I'm not doing anything—directly or indirectly—to make you want me."

I rub his shoulders. "Boy."

"Yes, Daddy?"

"I didn't think you were, even for a second. I'm in lust with you. The desire is all mine. I'm choosing to embrace it, to let myself want you. To let myself have you. The only thing you're doing is accepting me as your lover."

"I'm in lust with you too, Daddy. Which is why I'm desperate to taste your cock." He looks up and pouts adorably. "And when I've shown you how talented my mouth and tongue are, maybe you could pound my arse again."

I sigh and stroke his cheek. "You're crediting me with too much energy again." Sadness steals the burning heat from my groin. "Wouldn't you be happier with someone younger than me? Someone with more stamina and a shorter recovery period?"

Brin stares into my eyes. "No. I want you, Daddy."

The fire reignites, chasing the cold away. "That's good to know, boy."

He rests his cheek on my chest again. "You're the only man who's wanted to do nothing but hold me and chat. It's going to take some getting used to. I guess part of me thinks a man could only want me for one thing."

"Sex."

"Yes. Which isn't to say I don't want sex. I love sex."

I laugh, even though his words make my chest ache. "I'd noticed."

"But it's nice to be wanted in other ways too."

"Would you like to shower and watch a film? You could show me one of your favourites."

"I'd love that, Daddy." He walks his fingers down my chest towards my groin. "After I've sucked your cock?"

My pulse quickens. Blood rushes to my cock, making it hard. I can't resist him, nor do I want to. "Deal."

He grins, slides down the bed, and sucks my cock.

I an spends a lot of time at Nethermire over the next few weeks. With me.

He spends a lot of time with me.

I love every second of it. Whether that's enjoying each other's bodies and turning each other on, cuddling, watching a film, exploring the house and garden, or having tea with Mother. Ian is caring and attentive. It's the small things that make me smile, such as the way he'll absently stroke my back between my wings whenever he's beside me or the possessive way he puts his arm around my waist and his hand on my hip. The way he kisses me. The way he calls me boy, his voice deep and gravelly. The way he shows me, day after day, that he wants me. They're all things I never thought I could have.

How long will it last? I shouldn't ask myself that question. I should live in the moment and enjoy Ian while he wants me.

He arrives a little after seven. I run out the front door to meet him with a kiss and a hug.

"Hello, boy. I like that you're eager to see me." He loops his arm around my waist, tugs me against his bigger, stronger body, and kisses me passionately.

Heat rises to my cheeks. I hope Mother is looking out the window.

"I'm always eager to see you, Daddy. How was work?"

"Long but rewarding."

"Are you tired? Do you want me to get you anything? Tea? Cakes? A blow job?"

He chuckles. "I have a different idea." He leans against the car and hugs me close.

"Oh?"

"Correct me if I'm wrong, but I don't think anyone has ever taken you on a date."

"Uh, no. No one's wanted to, plus it's a little hard when I can't leave Nethermire."

"I want to." He uses his fingers to tilt my chin up and kisses me tenderly.

Warmth flashes through me. "Thank you, Daddy."

I appreciate the thought, even if he can't take me out for a meal, to the cinema, or whatever else people do on dates. My knowledge of dates, like everything else, comes from the things I've seen and read. You'd be surprised how many dates are ruined by serial killers, catastrophes, or villains.

Ian pushes me away gently and opens the car boot. He lifts out a large wicker hamper. "How does a picnic in the garden under the stars sound?"

Romantic.

"I wouldn't normally opt for a picnic in late autumn," he says.

"I can keep you warm."

"I know." He pinches my chin and kisses me. "Let's go."

He threads his fingers through mine, and we walk through the garden until we find a spot where we have a clear view of the night sky. Ian sets the hamper down, opens it, and retrieves a large picnic blanket, which he spreads on the ground.

"Sit, boy."

I obey, feeling a little useless but also very spoiled as he puts out the feast he's prepared. Sweet delicacies outweigh savoury ones, which suits me fine. He's packed a lot in the basket, including a bottle of wine and glasses. He sits beside me, his breath frosting in the air. Even though he's wearing a coat, he shivers. I snuggle up to him so that he can share my warmth.

"This is amazing, Daddy, thank you."

He kisses my forehead. "Anything for my bratty boy."

I snort. "Can I be bratty during a picnic?"

"Hm, I'm sure you'll find a way."

I lean forward and grab a long, thin cake with lots of icing.

"You're supposed to start with the savoury and end with the sweet, boy."

"Why?"

He opens and closes his mouth a couple of times. "That's how it's done."

"Humans are strange." I eat the cake as seductively as I can, making sure to get icing over my lips and chin so I can use my tongue to lick it off. "This is so good. Let me feed you one." I pick up another and feed it to Ian.

He eats it more slowly than I did, taking his time and not making a mess until I smoosh the last piece of cake against his lips.

He laughs and collects the sticky crumbs with his fingers. "I knew you'd find a way to be naughty." He slips his fingers into my mouth.

I stare into his eyes and suck the cake remnants off his fingers, using my tongue as though I'm pleasuring his cock.

"You are so sexy." He takes his fingers from my mouth and kisses me, his lips sticky and sweet.

"So are you, Daddy."

He takes a mini quiche, leans on one hand, and stares at the night sky as he nibbles his food. The sky is inky dark, with millions of stars scattered across it.

"I tried to paint stars once," I say.

"Oh?"

"Painting is one of the many, many hobbies I've tried over the years. It's the one I come back to the most, even though I'm no good at it."

"Oh?"

"It makes me feel close to Father. He painted all those portraits of Mother. I wanted to get good enough to be able to pain one of her too, but my efforts are childish at best. It's not something I have a talent for."

Ian hands me a cucumber sandwich with the crusts cut off. "How did you paint stars?"

"With white paint and a dry brush. I tried to splatter stars onto the canvas but ended up with more paint on me than anywhere else."

"I would have liked to have been there to clean the paint off you."

I laugh. "This was forty years ago. You'd have been five."

He nuzzles my neck before getting a sandwich for himself. "I still find it hard to wrap my head around the fact you're older than me."

I shrug. "Demon. I had much better luck learning and memorising all the constellations."

"Because your mind is a sponge?"

I grin. "Yes."

"Point them out to me."

"All of them?"

"Maybe not all of them, but your favourites."

I point out constellation after constellation to him as we eat. From Aquila to Canis Major, and Cygnus, the Northern Cross, to Lyra, Orion, and Ursa Major and Minor, and lots more in between. His gaze never leaves me, and he has a content smile as I speak. He makes me feel like I'm the centre of his universe.

"Fascinating." He hands me a cake. We're running out of food.

"Really?"

"Yes. I knew a few of those constellations, like Orion."

I giggle. "Everyone knows Orion. It's one of the easiest constellations to spot."

"Exactly." He claims my lips with his own. "Your enthusiasm was contagious. I'd love to stargaze with you again." He opens the bottle of wine and fills the glasses. "There's something goofy I've always wanted to do. Would you humour me?"

"Sure. What is it?"

"Link arms with my partner's while we drink our wine. Like this." He loops his forearm around mine. We have to lean close to each other to be able to sip the wine.

I laugh as I spill some down my chin. He wipes it away with his thumb and sucks it off. I pout. He could have let me suck it off his thumb.

"You're right. This is goofy," I say.

"And romantic. I hope."

I meet his gaze. "Yes."

We take a few more sips before unlinking our arms and putting our glasses down. Ian tidies the empty plates and containers into the basket.

"Can I help, Daddy?"

"No. I'm taking care of you, boy."

Once he's done, he puts his arm across my body, holding my shoulder as he encourages me to lie on my back. I stretch my wings over the blanket. Ian lies beside me. I curl the wing he's lying on so it half covers him.

"This is an amazing date. Thank you, Daddy."

"You're welcome, boy." He lies on his side, kissing me behind my ear and nibbling my jaw and neck. "Are you bored of me yet?"

I turn my face towards him. "I don't think I'll ever get bored of you."

"That's good. I like coming here and seeing you."

A few weeks ago, I'd have made a glib comment about how he enjoys fucking me. Which he does. There's no doubting that. But at this moment, it feels trite, like I'd be denying the meaning behind his words.

"Me too."

"Can we make this thing between us a bit more official?"

I frown. "In what way?"

He takes a small box out of his pocket and opens it. Inside is a thin silver chin with a circle on it. "It's a day collar."

"A—what?"

"I thought you'd read all about kink."

I wrinkle my nose. "That would have taken longer than one night."

"A collar is a symbol of commitment between a Dom and their submissive. Often, they are proper collars."

"Like a dog or a cat would wear?"

"Designed for humans, but yes, like that. But some people prefer something more subtle. Something they can wear all the time."

"Commitment?" I whisper.

"Confirming I want to be your Daddy and you want to be my boy."

I swallow. "For more than sex?"

"Lots more." He pecks my lips. "I want to take care of you, Brin."

"I want that too, Daddy." I turn my face away.

"But—?"

"But I'm stuck here. You don't need to be. You could find someone free to go where they want. Someone you can take on dates. Someone human."

He puts his fingers on my cheek and turns my face so I'm staring at him. "I want you, Brin."

"Why?"

He raises his eyebrows. "You're captivating, sexy, and fun to be around. I feel alive when I'm with you. I want you in a way I've never wanted anyone before." He kisses me. "I can't explain it better than that. I adore how bratty and chaotic you are. I've enjoyed every moment we've spent together. The sexy ones and the quiet ones. You're like a drug I can't get enough of."

"You know how to make a boy feel good about themselves."

"The collar is simply a way of saying we want to continue seeing each other."

Right. He's not asking me to marry him. Why would I even think that? We've only been screwing for a few weeks.

"So you're asking me to go steady with you?"

He laughs. "Have you been watching sixties movies?"

"I might have watched *Grease* this morning. The songs are very catchy."

"Yes, boy. I want to go steady with you. Will you wear the collar?"

I nod and tremble as he takes it out of the box and fastens it around my neck. I touch the metal. It's cool for about half a second before my body heat warms it.

"It looks good on you."

I grin and snuggle up to him. My gaze drifts to the stars. "Do you have work tomorrow?"

"No."

"You could stay over."

It's the one thing he hasn't done.

"I didn't bring spare clothes with me."

"Mother kept all of Father's clothes. They're dated, but they'd fit you. Sixties fashion would be appropriate, considering we've agreed to go steady."

He laughs. "I'd love to stay the night."

I look at him. "You could do all those things you talked about."

"Holding you all night?"

I nod as an odd fluttering sensation manifests in my chest.

"Waking up in each other's arms?"

"Yes."

"Making you breakfast."

I click my fingers. "Damn, you figured out my cunning plan. I want you to stay so you can be my breakfast slave."

"But not your sex slave?"

"Oh, that too. You can be both, right?"

He kisses me. "I can look after you in every way you need me to."

I nuzzle against his chest. "I know you can. Thank you, Daddy."

THE HOUSE IS dark and quiet when we return to it. Mother must be asleep. Unsurprising, considering it's nearly midnight.

I was amazed at how quickly the evening drifted by when all Ian and I did was cuddle, talk, and stargaze. It was the most wonderful first date I could have asked for and far more than I'd ever imagined.

He leads me to my room, sits on the edge of the bed, and pulls me between his spread legs.

I rest my forearms on his shoulders and gaze into his dark eyes. "Are you sure you want to date someone whose world is so small, Daddy?"

"Yes, boy. I wouldn't keep coming back for more if I wasn't okay with that."

"You're all right with it now. But will you be in another week? A month? A—" I bite my tongue. What's the point in thinking that far ahead? We had a few lust-filled weeks. I shouldn't imagine more.

"If it becomes a problem, I'll tell you." He nudges my T-shirt up and strokes my hips above the waistband of my jeans. "But I don't see why it should. As you keep telling me, this is a big house. The gardens are stunning, and then there's the main attraction."

I tilt my head. "The main attraction?"

"You, boy."

I smile. "What if you get bored of me?"

"To quote someone very special to me, I don't think I'll ever get bored of you."

I stick my tongue out.

He drags me to him, capturing my lips and tongue in a passionate kiss that makes my toes curl. I spread my wings and swish my tail around my body to stroke his calf. I dig my fingers into his shoulders, clinging on out of fear my knees might give way.

As he releases me, I gasp and bow my forehead to his. "I sometimes wonder how Mother has coped all these years, stuck here with me."

"She loves you, Brin."

"I know. But she gave up her whole life to look after me and keep me safe. How can I ever repay her?"

"I doubt she needs you to. I can attest to the fact that taking care of you is its own reward."

"Well, it's different with you. I can think of lots of ways to repay you for being amazing."

"True." He steers me so I'm sitting on his lap, facing him. "Have you ever tried to leave?"

"Yes. It hurt. A lot. I was bed-bound for several days."

Ian winces.

"Mother was so upset, although she tried to hide it from me. But I was young and fed up with being caged up here. I wanted to explore the world. Meet people. Do things that can't be done within the confines of a house and its garden. The internet opened the world up a lot for me. Virtual reality has let me experience some things, but only via two senses. It's not the same."

"No. It's not. And now? Do you still want to leave?"

"I've come to terms with having to stay here. But that doesn't mean I want to force anyone to remain here with me. If Mother wanted to go, I wouldn't stop her. I even told her to leave once. She cried." I sniff as a tear trickles down my cheek.

Ian wipes it away with his thumb. "Your tears are hot."

I let out a sad laugh. "Are you surprised?"

"I shouldn't be. Martha wants to stay. So do I." He brushes my hair away from my eyes.

"I'm sorry for bringing the mood down."

"You didn't, but I don't like seeing you sad. What can I do to make you smile, boy?"

"Hm, I can think of a few things."

"Do they all involve sex?"

I bob my head from side to side as I pretend to consider his question. "Yes."

"Or I could tickle you." He moves his fingers quickly and lightly up and down my sides.

I giggle and squirm and pretend to attempt to escape. He puts his hand on the small of my back and pushes me down his lap so we're chest to chest, and I'm sitting over his cock. He must be able to feel mine too, hard and wanting.

"That's better. Your smile is beautiful." He kisses me hard before I can say a word.

I smile against his lips and then part mine to invite his tongue into my mouth. He slides his hand up my back, beneath my T-shirt, and rubs between my wings harder than normal.

I tear my lips from his in a gasp, arch my spine, and let my head fall back. "That's so nice, Daddy."

He leans forward and kisses my exposed neck while he massages that sweet spot between my wings. "Is touching you there turning you on, boy?"

"You're turning me on, Daddy. But yes, it's so nice." I press into the touch.

"Demons have more erogenous zones than humans."

I shrug. "Who knew?"

He presses harder.

I groan and close my eyes so I can concentrate on my sense of touch above all else.

"Could I make you come from this alone?" He undoes my jeans and pulls my aching cock free of them. He's given up commenting on the fact I don't wear underpants.

He keeps massaging the sweet spot between my wings. He uses

his other hand to cup my neck and jaw. He kisses my lips, my throat, and the dip between my collarbones. I'm powerless to reciprocate, unable to move as I succumb to pleasure. I show my enjoyment in a string of moans, groans, and needy gasps. My wings twitch and shiver as pressure bears down on my groin. My balls draw up tight. They're so heavy they feel like they're going to explode. My last rational thought is that I'm going to make a mess of Ian's clothes. I gasp, shudder, and shake as my orgasm bursts out of me, painting Ian's shirt in white.

"Not quite stars," he muses, looking down at himself.

I laugh hard. "Not even close." I slump forward and rest my forehead on his shoulder. "That was amazing, Daddy."

"Ready for more?"

"Yes."

"On your knees, boy."

I obey without hesitation. I look up as he stands and takes his clothes off. He sits, legs splayed, and gestures for me to move between them. I know what he wants, so I grip his cock at the root, open my mouth, and take him deep.

He groans and grabs my hair in his fist. "Oh, boy, that's so good. Daddy appreciates that his boy has no gag reflex."

It's true. I don't. I can take him as deep as he wants me to. I'm unsure if it's a perk of being a demon or a perk of being me, nor do I care. All I know is my ability to take him right to the back of my throat makes him happy. I stroke his thighs as I bob my head up and down, sucking hard as I twirl my tongue over his hard, veiny length. Still grasping my hair, he uses his other hand to caress one of my horns. I whimper and moan around his cock.

"Stroke yourself, boy."

I put my hand between my legs and do as I'm told. It won't be long before I come again, but I know that's the point.

"Look at me."

I look up without releasing him from my mouth. Our stares

collide, his radiating something I can't name. My orgasm slams into me, and it's all I can do to keep sucking him off while I shiver and come all over the floorboards.

He pulls my head off his cock. "You're such a good boy."

I grin. "I thought I was naughty."

He chuckles. "You are naughty. But you're very good at turning me on."

"I try."

"Stand."

I get to my feet and remain still as he undresses me. He stands and pulls me into his arms, our needy bodies thrumming against one another. He picks me off my feet, turns, and lays me on the bed. My wings are fanned out beneath me. I'm still shivering from my orgasm, despite being more than ready for another.

Ian retrieves the lube, pushes my legs apart, and kneels between them. He runs his hands down my calves and then lifts my legs, hooking them over his powerful shoulders and raising my arse off the bed. He squeezes lube over my crack and hole and then uses a thick finger to warm me up. I stroke his leg, side, and arm with my tail while he pleasures me. It's the least I can do and the only way I can reach him.

"Stroke yourself," he commands.

"You want me to come again."

"Yes." His voice is low and husky. "I love watching you come undone, boy."

"It's a good thing I can come as often as you want me to, isn't it?"

"Very good." He leans down and nips my throat between his teeth before licking the hurt away from the same spot.

He kneels tall and inserts a second finger into my arse. He pummels back and forth with fervour, the pads of his fingers teasing my sweet spot over and over. I jack myself off with the same speed and intensity. When I come, he captures my cum in his hand and pushes the hot, sticky substance inside my arse.

"Damn, you're beautiful."

I tut. "Are ex-priests allowed to swear?"

"About as much as I'm allowed to fuck a sexy demon." He winks and thrusts his fingers so deep inside me my vision blurs for a second.

"I want you, Daddy, please."

He withdraws his fingers, sets my feet on the bed, with my knees bent, and lies over me. He kisses me and enters me gently. Then, supporting his weight on his hands, he stares into my eyes as he thrusts his hips slow and deep. I hook my legs around his waist, crossing my ankles so I can pull him deep inside me. I caress his face and coax his lips to mine for sweet kisses. Each thrust elicits a tiny gasp from me. I move my hips to greet his.

"Daddy," I whisper.

He smiles, dips his head, and runs his lips over the necklace he gave me.

I stroke his nape and tickle his spine. "What are we doing?"

"Making love." He kisses me hard, deep, and slow.

I close my eyes, losing myself in him.

Making love.

I come with a soft whimper, splashing hot cum between us. He keeps making love to me, keeps kissing me, his movements slow, measured, and perfect. I want this experience to last forever.

He grunts as he picks up the pace. He's about to come. I stare into his eyes as he groans through his orgasm. I come again too. Coating myself with my cum as he fills my insides with his. Panting, chest heaving, he lies over me and peppers my face with kisses.

"That was amazing, Daddy."

"You're amazing."

"Don't let me go," I whisper. "Don't pull out. Stay like this all night."

"Inside you?"

"Yes. With your arms around me. Show me I'm yours, Daddy. That I belong to you and no one else."

He chuckles against the crook of my neck. "You are mine." His tone is fierce and possessive. "Don't ever forget that."

"I won't, Daddy." I touch the chain around my neck. How could I?

IT'S light outside when I wake. Ian is lying over me, his beard tickling my shoulder. His cock is still deep inside me, no longer as flaccid as when we fell asleep.

His eyes flicker open. "Morning, boy."

"Morning, Daddy."

He cups my cheek and kisses me like he owns me. He does. I'm his. I know I joked about making him my sex slave, but I'd gladly be his, especially if I get rewarded with tender moments, picnics, and kisses. Especially if he keeps looking at me like I'm the most-prized possession in the world.

He moves inside me, making himself harder as he makes love to me with the same slow tenderness as last night.

"Daddy." I gasp and bare my neck so he can kiss my throat.

I rake my nails over his back. He claims my mouth, kissing me as though he owns me. We come quickly, our bodies shuddering as one. We lie still, enjoying each other for a long time.

"I promised I'd make you breakfast."

"We should shower first, Daddy."

"We probably should."

We make ourselves decent enough to cross the hall to the bathroom and then lock ourselves inside. We stand under the shower and wash each other with soap before I get on my knees and suck him off. He's not rested enough to come again, but that's not the point. When we're done, I fetch him some of Father's clothes, and we get dressed.

"How do I look?" he asks.

"Very dashing."

He's wearing pale trousers with sharp lines down the front and a short-sleeved shirt with a garish geometric print.

"Fashion in the sixties was interesting," he says.

I laugh. "You look great. You mentioned breakfast?"

"Judging by how you feasted on my cock, it's second breakfast for you." He spanks my arse as he chases me out the door.

"Oo, does that mean I'm a hobbit?"

"You've read a lot, haven't you?"

"Tons."

We go to the kitchen, and I sit at the table while Ian makes breakfast. When he's done, he puts two plates on the table. One has plain old toast on it. The other has toast covered in something white and hundreds and thousands. He pushes that plate to me.

"You said you liked sweet things, so I made you fairy toast."

I arch an eyebrow.

"Or my version of it anyway. Toast, covered in marshmallow spread with—"

"Hundreds and thousands." I lean over the table and kiss him. "I love it, Daddy." I pick up a piece and stare at him as I eat, purposefully making a mess with the marshmallow spread. It's deliciously sweet.

"Mal?"

I jerk my gaze towards the doorway, where Mother is standing, her trembling hand raised to her mouth.

Her shoulders sag, and her eyes dance with tears. "Oh, it's you, Ian."

"I lent him some of Father's clothes." I hang my head. "I'm sorry. I should have asked first."

She hobbles over to me and squeezes my shoulder. "It's fine. It's nice to see them put to use."

"I hope it was okay that I stayed over," Ian says.

"Of course. It's wonderful to see the two of you spending so much time together." Her stare falls on my necklace. "This is new."

"It was a gift from Ian." My cheeks blaze. She doesn't need to know more than that. "He asked me to go steady."

"Go steady?" Mother laughs. "I haven't heard that turn of phrase in decades." She ruffles my hair. "I'm so pleased for you both."

"Would you like some toast?" Ian asks.

"Maybe some coffee. Brin, would you mind?"

"Of course." I get up and make her coffee, warming the water to the perfect temperature by cupping the mug in my hands.

"Thank you, sweetheart." She sips her coffee as she stares at Ian. "Does that mean we'll be seeing even more of you?"

"I'm here a lot as it is."

"You're welcome whenever you want, dear."

"Thank you."

Mother finishes her coffee and then stands. "I'll leave you two lovebirds alone."

"You don't have to go," I say.

She chuckles. "I know I don't have to, but I'm certainly not going to stay and cramp your style. Enjoy each other. This stage of a relationship is a precious time. Savour every moment of it." She kisses my forehead. "I love you."

"I love you too, Mother."

She nods to Ian and then shuffles out of the kitchen, closing the door behind us.

"What do you want to do today?" Ian asks.

I grin and move to sit on his lap. "I can think of a few things."

"Let me guess. They involve sex?"

I gasp. "Not all of them. Have you ever done pottery?"

"Pottery? No."

"It's one of the hobbies I tried to take up. I even have a pottery wheel." I walk my fingers up his chest. "Did you know one of my favourite movies is *Ghost*?"

"I do now."

"Have you seen it?"

"Once, about thirty years ago."

"Do you remember the pottery wheel scene?"

"Yes."

I peck his lips. "How would you feel about recreating it? Naked."

A laugh rumbles in his chest. "I would love to, boy."

T stroke Brin's hair until his eyes open. He whimpers, moans, and flicks his gaze towards the window. It's still dark outside.

"What time is it, Daddy?"

"Early, but I have to go."

"Work."

"Yes."

I've spent more and more time at Nethermire since collaring Brin. Most nights, I'm reluctant to leave, and he never chases me away, instead enticing me into his bed with a mischievous grin and promises of naughtiness. At first, I resisted on nights when I had to be at work the next day, but after a few weeks, my resolve failed completely, and I started keeping an overnight bag in the car. Now, it's been at least two weeks since I've spent a night in my own flat. I adore falling asleep with him too much. Love waking up with him in my arms even more.

"I wish you could stay, Daddy."

"Me too. I'll come back later." I kiss him tenderly and ghost my palm over his nipple.

He gasps as it hardens beneath my touch.

"A promise of what's to come later, boy."

I kiss my way from his mouth to just above his groin, my lips fluttering over his tawny skin. Each barely there touch makes him shiver and moan.

"Stunning."

"Daddy." His voice is a keen. He pulls me up, wraps his arms around my shoulders, and demands hot kisses.

I give them to him gladly, wanting nothing more than to lose myself in him, even though I know I can't.

"I have to go."

Brin sighs and releases me. He flops one arm on the bed, over his wing, and the other over his forehead. He spreads his legs as I leave, an invitation for me to be naughty and stay. But I can't be late for work. I have patients who rely on my visits.

"I'm going to shower."

"I'll be here when you get back."

I hurry through the shower. When I return to the bedroom, Brin is where I left him, only now he's stroking his cock.

"Naughty," I say.

"You like it when I'm naughty." He releases his dick, sits, presses the soles of his feet together, and clasps his ankles. "I've been thinking."

"Oh?"

"When we first got together, you said you liked spanking naughty boys."

"I do."

"But you've never spanked me, and I'm very naughty."

I lean on the bed and kiss his forehead. "I like your brand of naughtiness too much. Why would I want to squash it?"

He grins, which is the most endearing sight in the world. I kiss his lips and then reach for my clothes.

"I want to know what it's like to be spanked, Daddy."

I pause halfway through putting my tunic top on. "You do?"

"Yes. It's something you like doing to your submissives." He touches his collar. "And well, I'm your submissive. Your boy. And I want to make you happy. So I want you to spank me."

I cup his cheeks in both hands and stare into his fiery eyes. "Are you sure?"

"Yes. If I don't like it, I can use those safewords I've never got any use out of."

"Yes, you can. Damn, Brin. How am I meant to go to work with thoughts of spanking your arse in my head?"

"You could call in sick."

I rest my forehead against his. "I can't."

"I know. Which is why you're going to go to heaven, and I'm—" He looks away sharply.

I stroke his cheek with my thumb. "I'm going to work and then coming back here to be with you."

"And to spank me?"

I chuckle. "Yes, boy, if you still want me to. I need to go." I pull away from him and finish getting dressed.

I'm halfway out the door when my phone buzzes with an incoming text. I fish it out of my pocket and pinch my brows together as I read the message from Mum.

"Is something wrong?" Brin asks.

"No. Dad has decided to throw a last-minute birthday party for Mum. This weekend."

"You have to go."

"I could tell him it's too short notice."

Brin gives me a stern look. "As much as I would love to have you screw me senseless all weekend, you need to go to your mum's party."

I cross over to him and kiss him. "Thank you for understanding."

"I'd be a crap boyfriend if I didn't. Go to the party. And go to work."

I would love to take him with me so he can meet my family, but I'm not going to say so aloud. Brin already has insecurities around the topic of him being bound to this house. I don't want to exacerbate them.

"It'll give me a chance to tell them all about you. They know I'm seeing someone, but we haven't had a chance to have a long chat about you."

"What will you tell your parents about me?"

"Hm, that you're amazing. That you make me happy."

"While all that is true, I meant about why I'm not with you. Unless I'm not invited, which is fine. In fact, that would be great. You wouldn't have to explain anything."

I kiss his forehead. "You are invited."

"Oh. Then you need to tell them something, or I'll look like the world's most terrible boyfriend."

"I'll tell them you're busy with work."

"Makes sense." He pushes my leg. "Speaking of work, you need to go."

"I thought you wanted to keep me here."

"I do. But you put clothes on, so it's easier to send you away. Have a good day, Daddy. I'll see you later."

I leave the house as quietly as I can so I don't wake Martha. I toss my bag inti the boot of the car, get in, and drive slowly towards the gate. I told Briin a small white lic. I'll need to go home between work and returning in order to put laundry on and pack clean clothes. I stop far enough away from the gate for it to swing open, and get out of the car. Martha has given me the code so I can open and close it myself rather than having to buzz through to the house. It's a crisp morning. The air has a chill to it. I pull my coat tighter around me as I jog to the keypad and punch in the code. I return to the car as the gates open with their customary whine. I must remember to bring something to oil them with. I drive through. I still shiver every time, but at least I know it's because of the wards. I get out and hit the button that will close and automatically lock the gates.

When I turn, a man is standing in front of my car. I press my hand to my chest. My heart thuds.

"Lost again?" the man asks.

My brain takes a few seconds to tell me why he seems familiar. He's the man who was asking if Nethermire was for sale. The man with the cold eyes and an even colder smile.

"What do you want?"

"You know what I want. To speak to the owner of this fine house."

"It's not for sale." I yank my car door open, eager to leave, except the man is still standing in my way.

"How is the owner? Is she quite well? She must be old by now."

I shiver. "What do you really want?"

"To speak to Martha. That's all. A cordial conversation between old acquaintances."

I gesture to the intercom affixed to the gate. "There's the buzzer. Call and see if she wants to talk to you."

The man tuts. "You know I can't touch that."

My limbs turn to ice. Fuck. "Leave. Martha won't want to talk to you."

"She might if you persuade her."

"Fuck off."

"No manners. Never mind. I can wait. Humans are such fragile creatures. So vulnerable to the ravages of time. It won't be long now." He turns and ambles down the road, fading out of sight as though walking into a mist.

WHEN I RETURN AFTER DARK, I find Martha in the front reception room. She greets me with an affectionate smile.

"Good day?" she asks, gesturing to the tea.

It will be the perfect temperature. It always is. Thanks to Brin. I pour out two cups and hand her one.

"Yes, thanks. Where's Brin?"

"In his den. I'm sure you're eager to find him."

I sit in the chair adjacent to her. "Actually, I'm glad I caught you alone."

Her expression becomes guarded.

"When I left this morning, I encountered that man again." I keep my voice low.

"That—man?"

"The one who was asking about the house several weeks ago." Months ago now.

She draws her eyebrows together.

"Is he a—?"

"Demon." She stiffens and stares out the window.

"How did you know?"

"There's almost always one sniffing around, hoping I'll forget to renew the wards on Nethermire." She sighs. "I don't tell Brin about them, of course. I don't want him to worry. He needs to feel safe here. It's his home."

"Of course."

"He didn't hurt or threaten you, did he?"

I shake my head.

"Good. Ignore him, Ian. He can't get inside the grounds. He can't hurt Brin." Her hand trembles as she lifts the teacup to her lips.

"Are you all right?"

She seems more subdued than when I first met her. I've continued doing her regular check-ups, and while her blood pressure has been a little low at times, there's been nothing too concerning. Just an elderly woman getting older day by day. No amount of nursing training will allow me to do a damned thing about that.

"Yes. That wasn't the news I wanted to hear this evening."

"I'm sorry."

She waves her empty hand. "Don't be. You were right to tell me. I won't let any harm come to Brin."

"Is there anything I can do to help protect him?"

She shifts her gaze to me and smiles. "You really care about him, don't you?"

"Yes." More than I can put into words.

She puts the teacup down and leans across to pat my knee. "One day, I'll teach you how to strengthen the wards."

I raise my eyebrows. "Can't Brin do it? Not that I don't want to help. I do—"

She chuckles to cut me off. "No, he can't. I did try to teach him, but it was in vain. A demon can't use, strengthen, or banish the wards supposed to stop them."

I stare at my teacup. "That makes sense."

"Brin says you're visiting your parents this weekend."

"Dad's throwing a surprise birthday party for Mum."

"Lovely. Birthday parties were something Brin missed out on growing up. I tried, but when it's just the two of you—"

"I'm sure Brin appreciated everything you've done to make his birthdays special."

"I hope so. Maybe his next one can be even more special."

"We'll find a way together."

She smiles. "Speaking of Brin, you should go to him. I'll cook dinner later, but not before you two young men have had a chance to work up an appetite."

I stare at her, mouth open.

"Oh, don't look at me like that. I know what it's like to be young and infatuated with someone. Mal and I couldn't get enough of each other."

I clear my throat. I don't blush often, but a not-very-veiled conversation about sex with my submissive's mother is enough to make my cheeks blaze.

"Ian—" She presses her lips together and shakes her head. "Go to Brin."

I frown. "Were you going to say something?"

"It doesn't matter. Go."

I put my full teacup down and wander to the door. I pause and look back at Martha. She's staring out the window again, her expression sad in the dimly lit room.

I knock my fist against the door frame.

"Go," she whispers. "Brin needs you."

And I need him. I slip away, navigating my way to the reception room farthest away from this one, where Brin has his film and games room. He's sitting on the sofa, playing a first-person shooter game. The moment I walk into the room, he pauses the game, tosses the controller aside, jumps up, and runs to me. He greets me with a hug and a kiss, and I respond in kind, kissing him far deeper than he kissed me.

"Hello, Daddy. Did you have a good day?"

"Yes, boy. Did you?"

"Well, it was boring without you here, but I found ways to entertain myself. My wrist had several very good workouts." He winks.

"Playing games?" I ask in an innocent tone.

He rolls his eyes. "You know what I meant."

"Do I?"

He undoes the catch on my trousers. "I could show you what I meant, Daddy."

I put my hands into the back pockets of his jeans and squeeze his arse. "You could, but I thought you wanted a different kind of pleasure this evening. What was it you wanted, boy?"

"To be spanked, Daddy. Will you? Please?"

I pinch his chin. "How much do you want it?"

"So much, Daddy. I'll get on my knees and beg if you want. I could do something else while I'm down there." He tugs my trousers zip down.

I grip his hair and tug his head back slightly. "You are so naughty, boy."

"Which is why I deserve to be spanked."

I smash his lips to mine and swipe my tongue into his mouth, tasting his delicious sweetness. "Yes, you do. I've been looking forward to this all day."

"And yet you made me beg. Silly, Daddy. You could have been spanking me by now. How do you want me? Leaning over the back of the sofa? Over your knee? Oo, please put me over your knee, Daddy." He shifts from foot to foot, his eyes wide and bright.

"You're a little too eager."

"It's something I've not experienced before. I might hate it, but I might love it. Either way, it's new and exciting and something that will make you happy. Spank me, Daddy."

I can't resist him any longer. I grasp his hand and tug him to the sofa. I sit, undo his jeans, and yank them to his knees. "You want to be bent over my knee, boy?"

"Yes, Daddy."

I pull him over my lap and caress his bare arse. "You want me to spank you?"

"Yes, Daddy. Spank me. Spank me hard."

W hat is it going to feel like to be spanked? Nice? Sexy? No amount of reading or watching kink scenes on the internet has prepared me for this moment. A thrill runs down my spine. Being draped over Ian's knee is sexy, especially as our cocks are rubbing. I fold my wings tight against my back, but they're still in the way.

"Give me a moment, Daddy."

I half close my eyes and concentrate on shifting my form. It's not easy, considering my current position, so it takes longer than usual to change into my human form. Well, partially my human form. I let my horns, ears, and eyes remain demonic. They don't get in the way of anything.

"I'm ready now, Daddy."

He caresses my bare arse, warming my skin. "Use your safewords if you need to, boy."

"I will."

He draws his hand away from my skin and then spanks it down with a light thwack. It stings a little, making me wince. He rubs the painful spot, erasing the hurt.

"How was that?" he asks.

"All right." My voice has an unexpected hesitance to it.

"Could you explain?"

I pinch my lips together. Can I? "I'm not sure what I was expecting. I watched some kink scenes on the internet of people being spanked. They were so into it. It turned them on. It looked sexy. But it hurt."

He keeps rubbing my arse. "Some people get off on pain. Some don't. It's not something you're going to know until you try."

"But spanking a submissive turns you on, right? You get off on doling out pain."

"Not too much, but yes."

I wriggle over his lap. "Try again. I probably just need to get used to the sensation."

Ian stills his hand. "Or it's not for you."

"Maybe. But I don't think one spank is enough to decide either way. I'm all right, Daddy. I want you to continue."

He sucks in a breath. "I don't want you to feel pressured into anything."

"You're not. I asked you to spank me, remember? I'm also asking you to do it again. Please?"

He sighs. "All right. If you're sure."

"I am. Green. That's right, isn't it? That's how I'm supposed to use the safewords?"

He chuckles. "Yes, boy."

He strokes my arse cheek for a few more seconds, then lifts his hand and spanks me again, harder this time. I flinch and hiss. He spanks me on the other cheek, once more increasing the pressure. The sting is intense. My eyes prickle. I'm feeling lots of things. Turned on isn't one of them.

I hang my head. "Red."

He sets me on my feet, pulls my jeans up, fastens them, and then gestures to his lap. I sit with my back resting against his chest. He loops a protective arm around me and kisses my neck.

"I don't think pain turns me on, Daddy."

"That's okay, boy."

My chin trembles. "Are you disappointed?"

"In you? Never."

"But I let you down. I got you all excited and then bugged out."

"No. You asked to try something new and discovered it wasn't for you. You're allowed to want something and then change your mind. You're allowed to say no. If anything, I'm proud of you."

I blink. "Why?"

"For using your safewords. For understanding your limits."

I clench my fists. "But if you enjoy spanking a submissive, why would you want to be with one who doesn't enjoy being spanked? Why would you want to be with me?"

He hugs me tight. "I adore you. While it's something I enjoy, I don't need it. I do need you."

I sniff. "And I need you. Which makes me sound super needy."

He laughs against my neck before kissing me. "We can be needy together."

"Yes, please." I rest my hand over his. "Daddy?"

"Hm?"

"Thank you."

"What for?"

"Making me feel safe."

"Always, boy. Always. Does the game you were playing have a two-player mode?"

"Yes."

"Will you teach me how to play?"

"Of course." I get off his lap to retrieve a second controller, which I give him.

We sit side by side, focused on the TV screen for the next hour while we play through the early levels of the game. We laugh and steal kisses whenever there's a cut scene or a pause in the game. I glance at him often. He's sexy, beautiful, strong, caring, and understanding. I rest my head on his shoulder and smile.

"Is everything okay?" he asks, wrapping an arm around my shoulders. It makes it awkward for him to play, but somehow he grips the controller in both hands.

"Yes. Just thinking about how lucky I am."

He kisses my horn. "If you're lucky, so am I."

"Lucky. Needy." I lift my head and grin. "Horny."

He laughs. "You're always horny."

"I am. Do you think that's a demon thing or a me thing?"

"A *you* thing. And I adore you for it."

I pluck the controller out of his hands and toss his and mine aside before straddling his lap. "I'm bored of playing the game now, Daddy. I want to play with you instead."

He slides his hands into the back pockets of my jeans and tugs me closer so I'm sitting over his cock. "You want to work up an appetite before dinner?"

I play-nip the tip of his nose. "Or maybe I'll devour you instead."

Ian presses his finger over my lips. "We'll devour each other. But first, I need you to do something for me."

Unable to speak, I raise my eyebrows.

"Show me the real you. All of you."

I grin against his finger and let my concentration unravel so I shift into my full demonic form, wings, tail and all.

He lowers his fingers. "Better." He cups my jaw and ravishes my mouth, making me one hundred per cent sure I'm the luckiest demon on earth.

CHAPTER
SEVENTEEN
IAN

Despite Dad arranging the party at the last minute, many people are here. Family, friends, and people Mum used to work with. I've spent most of the evening chatting with Victor. We seem to be the only people here—except for kids—who haven't come with a significant other. I'm missing Brin more than I imagined I would. After all, I'm only away for a weekend. I'll see him after work on Monday. Yet we've spent so much time together recently that knowing I won't be cuddling up to him in bed tonight creates a hole in my gut.

The party is in the function room of a pub, local to my parents. I decided I needed air, so I wandered downstairs to the beer garden. It's too cold for many people to be out here. The air has a static charge, promising a storm, even though there are only wispy white clouds in the sky. I gaze at the stars, trying to recall all the constellations Brin pointed out to me during our picnic date.

"You look like you need a drink." Neil, my younger brother, hands me a bottle of Bud Light and sits beside me on the bench. "Anything you want to talk about?"

I sip the beer. "Missing my boyfriend, that's all."

"It's a shame he couldn't come."

"Yeah." I pick at the bottle label.

"Tell me about him. Brin, wasn't it?"

"He's amazing. Vibrant, full of life, totally chaotic." I chuckle and take another sip. "Sexy. He makes me feel alive."

Neil nudges my elbow. "You've got it bad."

"Yeah, maybe."

"And to think that once upon a time, you took a vow of celibacy."

I sigh and stare at the bottle. "I would have kept it too if I hadn't realised I was bisexual. I spoke to one of my fellow priests at the time. He said God had sent sexual thoughts of men to test my faith."

"Is God meant to be an arsehole?"

"No. His statement didn't sit well with me. Why would God test any of us? If he's supposed to be all-loving, why would he reject any of us? Why would love have anything to do with whether or not we deserve to go to heaven?"

"Do you want my two cents? Bearing in mind, I'm about as religious as that rock over there." He points at a nearby flowerbed.

"Sure, go for it."

"The church gets its philosophies from the Bible, right?"

"Yes."

"And the Bible was written by people."

I nod.

"People are flawed. The people who wrote it will have had their own biases. The people who have interpreted the Bible over the centuries have their biases. What we're left with isn't the word of God but the word of man. I'm sorry the church couldn't accept you. But God will. Assuming he exists."

I take a long glug of beer. "How can you be sure?"

"If I recall correctly, there was a war in heaven because God wanted to give humans free will."

"That's what the Old Testament tells us."

"Why would he have given us free will if he didn't want us to forge our own paths, make our own decisions, and love freely?"

I shrug. My agnostic brother makes a good point.

Neil squeezes my knee. "Do you love him?"

"God?"

He laughs. "No, Brin. I assume you do love God."

"I thought I did."

"Until you had your crisis of faith?"

"Yes."

"You need to reassess what happened. Did you ever really doubt God or the church and its doctrines?"

"The church." I look to the heavens.

"I don't see how you can believe in something you can't prove exists. But that's me, not you."

"That's what faith is. Believing even without proof." I finish my beer and regard the empty bottle.

"Do you love Brin?" Neil asks.

"I—" I shrug. "I haven't known him long enough. I'm not sure what the future holds for us."

What can it hold for us? We could stay together for several more months, even years, but eventually, I'm going to grow old and die, and Brin will be left alone. His father found a way to stop Martha from ageing, but it wasn't permanent immortality, and she hasn't shared the secret with Brin. She might not even know what the secret is. Even if she did, would I want to be immortal? Would I want to remain forty-five forever while my parents, my brothers, and my niece and nephew all continue getting older? Am I stupid for even worrying about such things when the time we've been together is a drop in the ocean? Yet being with Brin is all-consuming. Thoughts of him fill my mind at all times. I want to be with him, want to hold him and protect him. Is that love or infatuation? Is there a distinction between the two?

"The funny thing about life is that we can't know what the future holds for any of us. That's the joy of free will and self-determination, of knowing our lives aren't controlled by fate. But not knowing what tomorrow holds is also fucking scary."

I chuckle. "It is."

"Which is why we need to make the most of each day. Admitting you love someone is scary, but it's worth risking your heart."

I squeeze Neil's shoulder. "You missed your life's calling."

"Oh?"

"You should have been a poet or a romance novelist rather than a lawyer."

"Who says I'm not a novelist on the side?"

I gape at him. "Are you?"

He laughs. "Nah. Like I'd have the time? When I'm not in court or preparing cases, I spend time with Laura and the kids. I don't have time for anything else. I don't want time for anything else. I'm happy. I'm pretty sure Victor's happy with his life too. The question is, are you?"

"Yes, I am. Things were shaky for a while when I left the church, but I've come to terms with that now. Yes, it left a gaping hole in my life, but I've mostly filled it with nursing."

"But something's still missing?"

I smile and tap the empty beer bottle against my thigh. "I don't feel like anything's missing when I'm with Brin. He makes me feel whole."

"Then I'll ask you again, big brother. Are you in love with him?"

"Yes. I am."

"Then my next question is, what are you going to do about it?"

"Tell him," I whisper. "And hope he feels the same about me."

"Is Ian coming today?" Mother is standing at the window, leaning on her cane, staring down the drive towards the gates. Not that the gates are visible from the house.

"Yes, after work."

It's Monday, and I haven't seen Ian since he left for work on Friday morning. I've missed him. It's like part of me has been missing. Ugh, I'm pathetic. We've been apart for three days. I'll be in his arms again in a few hours. Right now, I should focus on Mother.

I perch on the window ledge and touch her arm. "You look tired."

She smiles. "I am, a little."

"Are—are you all right?" My chest is tight as I speak.

She shifts her stare to me. "Yes, sweetheart. I need to replenish the wards. Would you join me?"

I always do, but— "Does it have to be today? Can't it wait?"

"I'm fine. Besides, I don't want to risk leaving them any longer. Any weaker and something might be able to slip through."

I shiver.

"Your safety is more important than me feeling a little tired. I'll replenish the wards and then have a nap. Come?" Mother never loses an argument. Not with me anyway.

"All right."

I take her arm, letting her lean on me rather than her cane, although she brings it with her. We take the same path we always do, around the outer perimeter of the garden via each of the cardinal points. Mother's voice is weary as she reels off the words that rejuvenate the wards. Are they spells? Incantations? Rotes? I'm unsure and have never asked. It's not as if the knowledge will help me do them.

"Mother, are you sure you're all right?" I must sound like a broken record.

She pats my hand. "Yes. Try not to worry, Brin."

"But I do worry." More and more.

"You don't need to."

I bite my tongue and look away. Is that true? She isn't like me. She's not immortal. She's not immune to human illnesses and diseases. Time is wearing her down, and there's nothing I can do about it.

"How did Father stop you from ageing?"

Her gaze becomes distant as she smiles. "By loving me."

"I love you, but you're still getting older."

"Do you want to know because of Ian?"

I frown. "What? No. I mean, maybe, one day. This thing between Ian and me it's—it's lust."

"Is it?"

"Yes."

"It's lasted a long time for something purely built on lust. If you and Ian become more serious, I'll tell you."

"Why not tell me now? Or sixty years ago? All these years, you've been getting older, and you won't tell me how I can stop it from happening."

She cups my cheek. "Oh, Brin. You can't."

"Why?"

"It's not something a child can do for their parent. I'm sorry."

I dip my chin. "I don't want to lose you."

"I'm not going anywhere yet."

"Ever. I don't want to lose you ever."

She rests her forehead against mine. "I know. I'm sorry. I don't want to leave you either. But it's not something we have any power over. Let's not worry about the future now, all right? I'm here, and we're happy, aren't we?"

"Yes."

"And Ian puts a grin on your face every time he visits. He's a lovely man. Open your heart to the possibility of more than lust, Brin."

We move on to the next cardinal point, and I wait while she strengthens the wards that keep me safe. I can't learn how to do them, but could Ian? Is that why Mother is so keen for us to feel more than lust for each other?

If I were to stay with Ian, it wouldn't be because he can do the wards instead of Mother. I feel safe in his arms. He makes me smile and laugh. I love raking my fingers through the thick carpet of hair on his chest. I adore the way his dark eyes sparkle whenever I say or do something that he would call chaotic or naughty. When he holds me, I feel invincible. He reassures me and lifts me up. I—

Oh.

"Brin?"

I blink slowly. "Am I—? Do I—? Could I?"

She tilts her head. "Love him?"

I nod.

"Yes."

"How did you know you were in love with Father?"

"Everything about him made me happy. The things he did and said. The small things he did to make me smile. When I woke up one morning and couldn't imagine my life without him, I knew I was in love. Can you imagine Ian not coming to spend time with you anymore?"

"I don't want to."

"Then that's your answer. You can be in love and in lust, Brin. The two emotions can and do go hand in hand."

"What do I do?"

She laughs. "Oh, sweetheart. You tell him."

"But what if he doesn't love me?"

She cups my cheek. "Then your heart will break. But it will mend over time."

Time. If there's one thing I'm not short of, it's time, unlike everyone else around me.

"I have a few more wards to strengthen. You can ponder how you're going to declare your love for Ian while I work."

We walk to the next cardinal point, which takes us past the front gate.

"Brin." Mother clutches my arm as she stares beyond the closed gate.

A man is standing on the other side. He's tall and gaunt with a pale face. He's dressed entirely in black, which makes his complexion even less healthy. His chin is sharp, his lips are thin, and his eyes are cold. One moment he's a man, like any other. The next, he has wings. Then they're gone. I blink and take a half step backwards. Is my imagination playing tricks on me?

"Martha." The man approaches the gate but doesn't touch it. "I was hoping to get a chance to talk to you." He shifts his stare to me and smiles. "But to meet your son as well? What a treat."

"Leave," Mother hisses.

"Brin, was it?" the man says, ignoring her. "What an *interesting* name. So very—human."

I grit my teeth and glare at him. "Who are you? What do you want?"

"Haven't you taught him anything?" the man asks, looking at Mother once more. "Such as how to recognise his own kind?"

He's a demon. My mind goes numb.

"I told you to leave," Mother repeats.

We're safe. He can't get through the wards. Mother is safe. I'm safe. He wouldn't hurt Mother, would he?

He steps towards the gate. "You look tired, Martha, and so very old. It won't be long now." He smiles at me.

I shiver.

"You will never get your hands on my son."

"We'll see, Martha. We'll see."

"Mother, let's go inside." I nudge her towards the house, but she stands her ground.

"Why won't you leave him alone?" she asks.

"You know why."

"He's done nothing wrong."

"He exists. Malagrok knew the rules and chose to break them. He has paid the price. His half-breed child needs to as well."

"Paid the— What did you do to him?"

"Oh, I'm sure you can use your imagination."

She shakes. I put my arm around her shoulders. When did she become so slender and fragile?

"Don't listen to him," I whisper. "He's trying to upset you. But we're safe here. He can't come inside the grounds. Let's go to the house. I'll make you some tea." I do my best to keep my voice calm, but it quivers despite my efforts.

She nods and lets me turn her away from the gate.

"He suffered," the man says. "Oh, how he screamed and begged for mercy."

I grit my teeth. "He's lying. Don't listen to him."

"We dragged out his suffering. Made him pay for disobeying us. And when you're gone, we'll make his son pay too. You're delaying the inevitable, Martha. You cannot save your son."

Mother presses her hand to her chest. She falters. I tighten my grip on her and hold her upright.

"Don't listen," I beg. "He's lying."

Is he?

Mother gasps. Her body stiffens and trembles. I struggle to keep her upright but am left with no choice but to lower her to the ground.

"Mother?" Tears sting my eyes.

She's fighting for breath. Her eyes are wide and unseeing. Her fingers claw at her chest. She's making terrible, rasping sounds.

"Mother!" I stare at the man. "What did you do to her?"

He steps back and spreads his arms wide. "Me? Nothing. She's old, Brin. I'll see you soon." He keeps walking backwards, slowly vanishing as if he were never there at all.

"Mother?" I put my hand on her cheek. "Breathe. Please breathe."

What do I do? I don't know what to do. I take my phone out of my pocket and ring Ian. The phone rings and rings and rings. Tears stream down my face. Mother is still making that awful noise, but it's quieter now. Fading. The phone flicks to voicemail. I ring him again. And again. And again.

"Brin? I'm with a patient. Is everything okay?"

"I don't know what to do." Can he understand what I'm saying through my sobs?

"Tell me what's wrong." His voice is calm, with a commanding hint to it.

Daddy has given me an instruction. "It's Mother. She's—she's struggling to breathe. She's holding her chest. I don't know what to do."

"I'll call an ambulance."

An ambulance. Of course. Why didn't I think of that?

"What can I do, Daddy? There must be something I can do."

"Make her comfortable. Talk to her. If she stops breathing, call me back, and I'll talk you through what to do."

"All right." I feel helpless.

"I'm on my way, Brin. I need to hang up now so I can call an ambulance. Okay?"

Nothing's all right. Will anything be all right ever again? "Yes, Daddy."

"I won't be long. I'm not far away." He hangs up.

I grasp Mother's hand and bow my head to it. "Please be okay. Keep breathing. Please." Sobs overtake me.

Talk. Ian told me to talk to her. So I do. I recount all my favourite memories we've made together until my throat is sore, my voice is hoarse, and a siren screeches towards us.

CHAPTER
NINETEEN

IAN

I pull onto the road that leads to Nethermire right after the ambulance. I follow it down the lane and park on the side of the road, out of the way, so the ambulance will be able to turn around and blue-light Martha to the hospital.

Brin and Martha are on the path, only a few footsteps from the closed gate. Somehow Brin is in his human form, despite the tears streaming down his cheeks and the fear etched on his face. He's sitting by his mum's side, holding her hand, talking softly.

I use the keypad to open the gate, letting the paramedics inside. At the same time, I fill them in on Martha's medical history and the medication she's taking for her arthritis.

"Brin." I kneel behind him and wrap him in my arms. "You need to let the paramedics do their job."

I gently detach his hand from Martha's and guide him to his feet. I lead him a short distance away and turn him around, using my bulk and height to shield him from seeing the paramedics work on Martha.

He stares up at me, his eyes flickering between dark brown and fiery red. "I didn't know what to do."

"You did the right thing calling me. The paramedics will help her."

"She can't die, Daddy. She can't." He tries to look around me.

I put my hands on his cheeks and hold him firm. "Look at me, boy."

He obeys.

"You need to let them do their job."

He nods. His chin trembles.

"What happened?"

"Mother was strengthening the wards. There was a man here." His voice is harsh and raspy. "No. Not a man. A demon."

Fuck. Was it the same man I'd seen a couple of times? The man I'd warned Martha about.

"He said horrible things about Father. He told Mother that—that —" He scrunches his face as his shoulders shake and shudder. He fists his hands into my coat.

I release his face so he can lean forward and cry against my chest.

"And then she—" He makes a helpless gesture with his hand before clinging onto me again. "She has to be all right. She has to be."

I wrap my arms around him and rub his back. I can't make him any promises. I glance over my shoulder. The paramedics are loading Martha onto a stretcher, as well as giving her oxygen.

"They're going to take her to hospital."

Brin looks up. "Will you go with her, please?"

My heart wrenches. I belong here, with Brin.

"Please, Daddy? I don't want her to be alone. I can't go with her." His face crumples. "Please. I don't want her to be alone."

"What about you? The paramedics, doctors, and nurses will take care of Martha. Who will take care of you?"

He pulls away and rubs his eyes with the heels of his palms. "I'll be all right as long as Mother isn't alone. Please, Daddy. Go with her."

I don't want to go. I want to stay and hold him. I want to take his pain and fear away. Only I can't.

"Please." His voice is desperate.

I blink back tears. "All right. I'll call you as soon as there's any news."

"Thank you, Daddy."

I kiss his forehead and then jog over to the paramedics, who have finished loading Martha into the ambulance. I confirm which hospital they're taking her to and then follow them out the gate, closing and locking it behind us. I look back before getting into my car. Brin is standing behind the gate, his stare fixed on the ambulance as it drives away from Nethermire. It's a wretched sight, one which makes my gut wrench. What is he thinking and feeling? Fear? Helplessness? Frustration? Anger? Why can't I tear myself in two so I can go with Martha and stay with him?

I CAN'T DO MUCH at the hospital except wait, but eventually, I get given the news I was hoping for.

I call Brin straight away.

"Daddy?"

"Martha is going to be okay."

"Is she awake?"

"Not yet. She needs to rest, Brin. She'll have to stay in the hospital for a few days at least while they run some more tests. But the prognosis is positive."

"Did they say what's wrong?"

"She had a stress-induced panic attack."

"It was so scary. I thought she—"

"I know, boy."

When Brin called me, I'd worried Martha was having a heart attack. Not that a panic attack isn't a scary thing, especially one of that scale, but there will be significantly less recovery time. I assume they want to keep her in the hospital due to her age and because she has no history of panic attacks. It's not as if she can tell them a demon goaded her to believe awful things had happened to her lover.

"You'll stay until she wakes, won't you?" Brin asks.

I can't deny him. "Yes."

"Thank you."

We talk for a little longer, and then I gather drinks and snacks before sitting at Martha's bedside. I could be in for a long night. I read a book until my eyes get too heavy to keep awake. Then I doze in the chair, despite the noise from the machines Martha is hooked up to and the ward outside.

"Brin?"

I jerk awake and stare around the darkened room. I'm in the hospital. With Martha.

"You're in the hospital. Brin's fine, other than being worried about you."

She reaches for my hand. "Ian."

"Brin asked me to stay with you. I hope that's all right."

"You need to go to him." She tightens her grip on my hand. "He's in danger. The wards—" She coughs and clutches her chest.

I reach for the call button, but she pulls me away.

"I didn't finish replenishing the wards. They'll be fading."

My heart races.

"I need to get back to Nethermire." She tries to sit, but her strength fails her. "You need to do it for me, Ian. Please. You can't let them take Brin away."

"I don't know what to do." My thoughts are woolly. My fingertips tingle. The room spins.

"I'll teach you." She tugs me close so my ear is close to her lips. "Listen."

I can't sleep. I have tons to do in the house—games to play, books to read, hobbies to do—but none of them hold my attention for more than a few seconds. Even knowing Mother will be all right, I can't shake the fear, worry, and panic that settled in my bones when she collapsed.

I lie on my bed. It's the one-hundredth time I've come here to close my eyes, clear my head, and sleep. It doesn't work. Could I have done something differently? Could I have chased the demon away? Could I have protected Mother?

The front door opens. I tense. Is it Ian? No. He can't bring his car up the drive without the tyres scrunching on the stones. Besides, he's at the hospital with Mother.

Oh no.

The wards.

Mother didn't replenish all the wards. She'd said they couldn't wait another day. Could they have weakened enough to let demons inside Nethermire?

Footsteps echo through the house.

My skin crawls.

I slip off the bed and sneak to the fireplace. I know exactly where to place my feet so as not to make a sound. I turn into flames, briefly feeding on the wood before drifting up the chimney.

My bedroom door opens.

"Come out, Brin. I know you're here." It's his voice. The demon who made Mother sick.

My flames flicker and crackle. I have to stay hidden. I won't be any match for a demon who knows the true extent of his powers.

"Why delay the inevitable? It was always going to end this way. We were always going to come for you. We were always going to take you home."

No. This is my home. I'm as much human as I am demon. This is where I belong.

A cold light radiates up the chimney's breast. "Ah, found you." His voice comes from all around me. The light drifts towards me.

I flee through the chimney system, turning this way and that, moving up and down the house in an attempt to outrun him. He's getting closer. My flames recoil from the cold pursuing me. I've got nowhere to go except out.

I spill out of a fireplace into one of the unused reception rooms. The one Ian and I first got sexy in. The demon bursts out after me, his light surrounding me. It stings and burns. His light is so cold. I wrest away from him, landing hard on the floor as I return to my demonic form. I run towards the door. Big mistake. It opens, and a huge demon bars my path. I stop too fast, lose my balance, and fall. The cold light floods over me, making me shiver and hiss. It feels like ice picks are tearing across my skin. The huge demon bends down, grasps my arms, and pins them to my sides as he lifts me like a rag doll. The cold light streams away from me, forming the demon who hurt Mother. I struggle, kicking and writhing in the big demon's grasp, but he's too strong.

The cold demon tuts. "I told you your fate was inevitable, Brin." He presses his thumb to my forehead.

Cold light flashes through my head. Every part of me becomes numb. I can't think. Can barely feel. My body flops in my captor's arms. Chilly darkness claims me.

Ian.

Mother.

I'm sorry.

I ACHE ALL OVER, and my head feels like it's stuffed with cotton wool. I whimper as I open my eyes. Not that it helps. I'm surrounded by impenetrable darkness. I can't even make out the outline of my hand as I hold it up in front of my face. Tormented screams drift towards me. My skin crawls. Welcome to hell.

I touch the necklace Ian gave me. It's still there, warm and comforting against my skin. I close my eyes and concentrate on recalling his face. His smile. His dark eyes. The way his beard tickles my chin and jaw as we kiss. I love him. I will see him again. But first, I need to figure out where I am and how to get out.

The ground is rough, hard, and warm. I get onto my knees and crawl forward, sometimes lifting my hand to see if my fingers graze against anything. I'd rather not smack face first into a wall, thanks.

"Come now, you can do better than that." The amused voice is unfamiliar. It echoes around me, coming from every direction at once.

I turn my head this way and that, even though I can't see a damned thing, let alone whoever's taunting me.

"Make your own light."

My own light. Right. I can turn into flames. I rock onto my heels, lift my hand, and concentrate on fingers I can't see. A moment later, flames flicker in front of me as I partially shift. The fire is enough to see my environment. I'm in a stone chamber without doors or windows. I'm in the very centre of it. Each curving wall is about twelve feet from me. The ceiling is equally high. I stand and walk towards one wall. My distance from it doesn't change. I run. It's still twelve feet ahead. It reminds me of one of the punishments in Tartarus, only very toned down. It's a lot better than having my liver pecked out by birds for the rest of eternity.

I stop and clench my corporeal hand. "Is this to be my prison?" I demand.

"Perhaps," the voice responds.

I glare at the cavern. "Why? What did I ever do?"

"You were born."

"So you're going to condemn me for something I had no control over? My big sin is existing?"

"Yes."

"Well, screw that. I have never done anything to hurt anyone. I've never stolen or cheated. Never lied or deceived. I've never got a human pregnant, and trust me, I never will. Tell me what I've done to deserve to be torn from my home and stuck in a tomb of rock. Tell me." My voice has risen to a sharp shout. My throat aches.

Silence responds.

I laugh. "You can't. I haven't done anything to deserve this. You've already punished my father. Why do you care about me? Why can't you let me live my life? I'm not going to run around showing humans that demons exist. I want to go home." I clench my teeth. No. I want more than that. "I want to be able to stop being afraid. I want to be able to explore the world. I don't want to be trapped in that house anymore. I don't want to be hounded by you and your minions anymore."

The voice chuckles. "Minions. I like that. Such a human concept."

"Exactly. I'm half human. I don't belong here." I belong with Mother and Ian.

"You talk a lot. I'm not used to being defied by my demons."

"Well, get used to it. If you keep me here, I'm going to keep defying you. I'll keep yelling and screaming at you until you get so fed up you beg me to leave."

The voice laughs, a booming sound that echoes around the cavern. "I don't doubt it."

"Then let me go. I can be very annoying when I want to be. And I'm stubborn. You wouldn't believe how stubborn I am. Let me go and live freely without the fear of your subordinates dragging me back here."

"And that's all you want?"

I bite my tongue before I blurt out a yes. "I want to know what happened to my father. What did you do to him? That cold demon said—he said—" I can't make myself say the words.

"Malagrok is not dead."

My legs give way, and I fall to my knees. My burning hand hits the floor as my concentration slips. My hand returns to normal, and I'm plunged into darkness once more.

"Thank you," I whisper.

"I don't understand."

"What? Why I thanked you?"

"Why you wouldn't want to stay here and discover your full potential."

"It'll be a bit hard to do that stuck in here." I narrow my eyes. "Unless I'm wrong, and that isn't what you're planning on doing."

"I'll keep you here for as long as it takes you to learn obedience."

"I can be obedient. But I'll never obey you." He—whoever he is—is not my Daddy. "I don't care about my full potential. I'm happy the way I am." I release a sad laugh. "Brin, demonic tea warmer at your service."

"You are a strange creature."

"Am I? You know what else I am? Annoying." I hug my knees to my chest and launch into a very loud, very out-of-tune rendition of 'I Know A Song That Will Get On Your Nerves'.

"What is that?" the voice asks.

I ignore him and keep singing. When I'm bored of that song, I stand and move on to the 'Macarena', complete with dance moves.

"Hey, you should send some of your minions in here. I'll teach them the dance."

"You are—"

"Annoying? Yes. Bored of me yet? I've lived on Earth for over sixty years. I know a lot of very annoying songs."

I repeat the song, throwing my all into the dance moves, even though I can't see a thing. Can the owner of the echoing voice see me?

"If you want me to stop, tell me what you did to my father. I'll be quiet while you do. No promises how noisy and irritating I'll be afterwards, though."

A sigh fills the cavern. There's a grating sound, and then hot red light pours into the cavern. I fling my arm up to shield my eyes. Something rumbles. The cavern shakes as something slams shut.

"Brin." This voice is warm and close. It comes from a single point in front of me.

I will my hand to turn to fire. The light I've created flickers and bounces around the cavern. I'm standing face to face with a tall demon. His hair is as dark as mine, his eyes as red, and his skin is a similar hue. He's broad and muscular. In human terms, he looks to be around thirty. He has a neat beard and a kind smile. His horns are longer and twistier than mine.

"Wh-who are you?"

He raises his eyebrows.

"F-Father?"

He nods.

I almost run into his arms but falter. Is this a trick?

"How is Martha? She used to love to sit in the morning room and tend to her plants. Does she still do that?"

My chin trembles. I go to him, press my head to his chest, and embrace me.

He wraps his arms around me. "I thought I'd never see you again."

"Did they hurt you?"

"No. My punishment was simply to remain here. I cannot traverse between here and the mortal realm anymore."

"So you'll never be able to see Mother again?"

"No." It's one word, but it's full of so much sadness.

"Come now, Malagrok. That's not the full truth. Is it? You could have gone back to your lover's side, but she forgot about you."

"That's not true," I yell. "Mother loves him with all her heart. You tore him from her." I stare at Father. "There isn't a day that goes by that she doesn't think about you or talk about you. She loves you."

He squeezes my shoulder. "I don't doubt that, Brin."

I frown. "What does he mean you could have gone back to Mother?"

Father turns away from me and bows his head. His wings, tattered at the edges, are folded firmly against his back. "I would have been allowed to leave and live the rest of my days on Earth if Martha had recalled me to her side."

"But she didn't," the voice says.

"Did anyone bother to tell Mother she could recall you?"

Father shakes his head.

"It was proof this mortal concept of love is worthless," the voice says. "If this woman had truly loved Malagrok, she would have stopped at nothing to be with him again."

"What kind of stupid, twisted logic is that? First, Mother probably didn't even know it was possible. Second, she spent every waking moment keeping me safe because your minions kept sniffing at our gate, waiting for her to let the wards slip so they could steal me away from her."

"If she'd truly loved your father, she would have found a way. Nothing would have kept them apart."

"You can't expect someone to win a game when they don't even know they're playing one. Your experiment was flawed at best and cruel at worst. You weighed the odds in your favour. You wanted Father to lose faith in Mother and in love, but I won't. Mother loves me. Ian loves me. Nothing you can say or do will convince me otherwise." I slice my arm through the air. "Human love is not worthless. It's the most powerful thing there is."

"So passionate. It's a shame your thinking is flawed."

"No. Yours is. You had to cheat to prove your theory." I step towards Father. "Surely, you know she would have recalled you if she'd known she could? Surely, you know she loves you?"

He turns and cups my cheek. "Yes, Brin. I know. I don't blame Martha for any of this. It was enough to know she was keeping you safe."

"D-do you still love her?"

He smiles. "Yes."

"I offer you the same deal," the voice says.

"What?" I ask.

"If these mortals you're so desperate to go back to love you truly, they'll summon you. Then you'll be free to live on Earth. None of my minions will—how did you put it? Sniff at your gate."

"And if they don't?" Father asks.

"You stay here for eternity, and you will obey me, even if I have to break you first."

"Just like that?" I ask. "Why should I trust you to keep your word? You won't even show yourself. How do I know you have the power to release me? For all I know, you're a prison guard on a power trip."

"Brin," Father says in a warning tone.

"Go on. Show yourself. Or at least tell me who you are."

"I am the master of hell."

I fold my arms. "I don't believe you. I've seen *Lucifer*. Your voice is nowhere near as sexy as his."

"Brat."

I stamp my foot. "Only one man gets to call me that, and it isn't you. You're a coward and a cheat. I will never respect you. Run along and fetch your master. I'll speak to him. I'm done wasting my time with a prison guard."

Pain tears through my head. I clutch my skull as I'm driven to my knees by the vision of something beyond my comprehension. Something epic and terrifying. Something ancient and powerful beyond belief.

"I am no prison guard, boy."

I spit words through my gritted teeth. "No one but Ian gets to call me that either, especially not you." I struggle to my feet. "I will not bow down to you. I will not cower before you. I will not be broken."

Wind rushes through the cavern. Father is torn from me in a rush of air.

"Brin!"

"Father!" My hand snaps back to being physical, plunging me into darkness. "Father?"

He doesn't respond. I'm alone. I concentrate on turning my hand to flames but can't. The voice wants me to give up. He wants me to despair. Well, I won't. I will never give up. Ian will rescue me. He will. I lift my chin, clench my hands, and sing 'My Heart Will Go On' at the top of my voice. The darkness deepens. I close my eyes against it and sing.

I will not give up.

I t's dawn by the time I reach Nethermire House. I don't shiver as I drive through the gates. Fuck. The wards must have already faded. When I pull up outside the house, the front door is open. I slam my fist against the steering wheel. I'm too late.

My heart thunders as I run into the house, calling out Brin's name. The only answer I get is silence. Even so, I check every room. Most are undisturbed, but I find a scorch mark on the floorboards in the room Brin and I first fooled around in. I crumple onto the sofa, hands clenched and shaking. I stare at the ceiling and scream.

I rest my elbow on my knee and drop my head into my hand. Martha told me how to renew the wards around Nethermire, but she didn't mention anything about what to do if it was already too late. Does she know? Probably not, or Mal would be here rather than rotting in hell.

I tug my hand through my hair and let out an ugly sigh. I won't accept Brin is gone. I won't accept that I'll never get to hold him again, never see his smile again, or roll my eyes at his bratty behaviour. Never get to make love to him again or hear him call me Daddy. That I'll never get to tell him I love him. If there's a way to get him back, I'll find it. I won't be left with nothing but memories of my bratty, vibrant boy.

I cup my hands over my mouth and take several deep breaths. I need to calm down and think clearly. Would a priest trained in exorcism be able to help?

No. Don't be ridiculous, Ian. They get rid of demons and ghosts. They don't summon them.

Summon.

I could summon him. Couldn't I? Is it even possible?

I take my phone out of my pocket, open a web browser, and type 'how do you summon a demon' into the search bar. I shouldn't be surprised when over thirty-eight million results are returned. I'm sure most are garbage, but I only need one of them to work. I'll click on all thirty-eight million results if I have to.

The first result is a blog entry by someone who finds making friends hard. They posit the question, why make friends when you can summon them? Why, indeed. According to the blogger, I need somewhere to perform the summoning, salt, scented candles—they insist lavender is best—lots of chalk, a box of matches, and an offering of some sort. They suggest chocolate. Under normal circumstances, that would spark alarm bells that this ritual is in no way going to work. But I'm a desperate Daddy, determined to recall his boy to his side.

I search the house for everything I need. I need to thank Brin for trying so many hobbies over the last sixty or so years. Using chalk as an art medium was one hobby he tried once, judging by how little the ones I find are worn down. He even tried candle making, though none of them are scented. They'll have to do. If anything, being made by Brin should make a positive difference. As for the offering—

Brin likes sweet things. I make fairy bread Ian style, with plenty of marshmallow spread and hundreds and thousands.

Once I've gathered everything, my next task is to find somewhere to draw the summoning circle. The blogger suggests a cellar or attic, or, failing that, somewhere spooky like a dark forest or an abandoned building. None of those suggestions are helpful. Nethermire House doesn't have a cellar, and the attic rooms are full of the things Martha has accumulated during her long life. I don't want to disturb any of them.

Brin's room. It's large and doesn't have much in it. I run up the stairs, my arm full of summoning paraphernalia, which I deposit on his bed before pushing it against the wall to maximise the floor space in the room.

What's next? Creating a circle of salt. I purse my lips as I read the blogger's reasoning. Demons can't cross salt. Is that true? It can't be true. I've seen Brin eat things with salt in them. If he couldn't cross a line of salt, he definitely couldn't eat it. Forget the salt. But if the blogger has that detail wrong, what are the chances this is going to work at all? I shake my doubts away. I have to believe. I have no proof it will work, but I have to have faith it will.

I follow the next step, which is to draw a large circle in chalk and a huge pentagram inside it. Put your heart and soul into it, the blogger says. I'm definitely doing that. I put a candle on each of the points and the sixth in the centre. I light the candles and place the plate of fairy bread beside the central candle. Next, I have to say—wait. What does *secular saeculorum* even mean? I open a new browser tab and find a translation. Forever and ever. Doubt tugs at my gut once more. This isn't going to work.

I go back to my original set of search results and scroll through them. wikiHow has a page on how to summon a demon. Figures. I skip past it. I read and disregard post after post, all of which seem more ludicrous than the last.

Eventually, I find a post with a summoning incantation in Latin that has a lot more meat to it than simply saying *secular saeculorum*. I don't recognise every word, but I've said mass in Latin once or twice in the past, so I do understand some of them. The warding incantations Martha taught me were also in Latin. Could this work? There's only one way to find out.

I clear my voice and speak slowly and clearly. *"Exude vocal meam, et intende supplicatio meam. Obsecro te inter mortal regnum et infernum transfer obicem. Brin."*

The candle flames flicker. For a moment, it feels as though the air has been sucked out of the room. All returns to normal, except for a slight static charge in the air.

I repeat the incantation, louder and with more conviction. I repeat them until my throat is sore and my tongue is heavy in my mouth. Each time I say them, the candle flames flicker more violently. After the sixth attempt, they climb high. The ceiling light buzzes and breaks, raining glass onto the floorboards. The room becomes hotter than a sauna, the air dry and caustic. It's hard to breathe. I repeat the incantation again. The air crackles. A ball of fire bursts into existence. I keep speaking, keep repeating the incantation, my mind focused on Brin. On bringing him home. The fireball grows in size, its heat almost unbearable. I raise my arms to shield my face, but my voice never falters. The fireball changes, forming the shape of a slender man with wings, horns, and a tail.

"Brin."

His form changes from flame to flesh and bone. "Daddy. I knew you'd find a way to get me back. I knew you would." He flings himself into my arms.

I hold him tightly. "Always, boy. You're mine. I'm never going to let you go. Never."

"I'll hold you to that, Daddy. I missed you."

"You've only been gone a few hours."

He draws back and winces. "Time works differently in hell. It felt like a lot longer." He gives me a weary grin. "I taught Lucifer—or whoever he was—several annoying songs while I was there. I don't think he liked me very much." He fists his hands into my shirt. "Is Mother all right?"

"Yes. She needs to rest, but she'll be able to come home soon." My heart stutters. "She taught me how to do the wards. I'd better—"

He presses his hand over my face. "No need, Daddy. Assuming the big boss man keeps his end of the bargain, I'm free."

I frown. "You are?"

"Yes. He was so convinced that love is a fallacy that he made me a deal. If you recalled me, he would set me free. And you did." He grasps my face and kisses me hard. "I knew you would. I love you, Daddy."

I lift him off his feet and swing him around. "I love you too, boy. I love you too."

I set him down and kiss him with fervour and passion. I kiss him with the force of my relief and love. I kiss him until our lips are bruised and swollen, and I'm breathless and giddy.

"Say that again. I don't think I heard you the first time," Brin says.

"I love you."

"Still can't hear you, Daddy."

I chuckle. "I love you." I'll say it a million times if I have to. "You're mine."

He sighs and cuddles against me. "Yes. I am." He looks up. "I saw Father."

I widen my eyes. "You did? Is he all right?"

Brin nods. "His punishment was to be forced to stay in hell. Only the demon in charge gave Father the same deal he gave me. He could be free if the person who loved him summoned him out of hell."

"Let me guess. He didn't tell Martha about the deal any more than he told me?"

"It was a rigged offer. I think—no, I believe—that if Mother hadn't been so focused on protecting me, she'd have stopped at nothing to rescue Father. Then again, if I hadn't been born, Father wouldn't have been punished in the first place. But it means there's still a chance we can rescue Father. That he and Mother can be together again."

"I'll summon him."

Brin shakes his head. "It has to be Mother."

I breathe out and nod. Of course it has to be Martha.

"I want you, Daddy," Brin whispers, his voice taking on a playful tone. "I was in hell for so long, and it was so terrible. The only thing that could possibly make it better is the healing power of my Daddy's dick."

I chuckle. "That can be arranged, boy."

He gives me an apologetic smile. "But I need to see Mother first."

"Of course." I lean down and kiss him. "My magical dick can wait. We're together. No one is ever going to tear you away from me again." I take his hand. "Let's go and see Martha."

BRIN STARES out the car window as we drive to the hospital. His eyes are wide, and he points things out with gleeful excitement.

"Oh! That's a telegraph pole. And look! There's a railway bridge. Can we go on a train soon, Daddy?"

I chuckle. "We can go anywhere you like."

He dances in his seat. "Wow. These buildings are so tall. And there are so many. I've seen cities in films and TV programmes, but I didn't realise how small I'd feel driving through one."

His reaction to all the sights and sounds brings me intense joy.

He becomes a little more subdued once we reach the hospital, clutching my hand as we walk through the busy corridors to her room.

She's sleeping. A monitor shows her heart has a steady rhythm. She's hooked up to a drip, which is giving her fluids and nutrients.

"Mother."

"It looks scarier than it is," I promise him. "She's going to be fine."

He nods, pulls up a seat, and sits by her side. He's holding her hand when she wakes a few minutes later.

"Hello, Mother."

Her eyes widen. "Am I dreaming?"

"No. I'm here." He stands, kisses her forehead, and then takes his seat again. "Ian's here too." He leans to one side so she can look past him more easily.

I'm sitting in a chair in the corner, exhausted but not willing to let myself doze off. I need to be here for Brin. I love him.

Mother squeezes Brin's hand. "How? I don't understand?"

"It's a long story. For now, all you need to know is that Ian saved me and that you can bring Father home. He's alive. He's all right."

Her chin trembles, and tears leak from her eyes. Her chest shudders as she sobs. Brin hugs her as best he can, and soon he's crying too. I sniff and rub my thumb under my eye. Family reunions always choke me up.

Martha stretches her free hand towards me. "You need to come over here, young man."

I chuckle and walk to the other side of the bed.

"You're part of this family now. Assuming you love my son as much as I think you do."

"I do. With all my heart."

"Then give me a hug."

I lean down and hug them both, massaging Brin's shoulder with my fingertips as I do.

"You're truly free?" Martha asks Brin.

"Yes."

"Then you'll need to make a list of all the things you want to see and do."

Brin laughs. "It'll be a long list."

"They're the best kind." She pinches his cheek and then coughs. "Brin, would you be a dear and fetch me a drink?"

He glances at the bedside table, which has a jar of water and a couple of glasses on.

"Something a bit more interesting than water. I'd love a cup of tea."

Brin purses his lips. "Where am I going to find good tea?"

"Go explore. I'm sure you'll find somewhere." She pushes him towards the door. "Go."

He narrows his eyes. "You're trying to get rid of me, aren't you?"

"Yes. But it's for a good reason. I promise." She points at the door.

"Fine, I'm going." He darts around the bed to kiss me and then slips out of the room.

I fold my arms. "What was that about?"

"I needed a moment alone with you. Pull up a chair."

I grab the chair I was sitting on and take it to the side of the bed I was standing on. I sit and fold my arms on the edge of the bed. "Is everything all right?"

"How do you feel about Brin?"

"I love him."

She smiles. "Do you think you might choose to be with him forever?"

I suck in a breath. Forever has very different connotations with Brin.

"It's not a simple decision. Believe me, I know. I had a family when I met Mal. Parents, sisters, and brothers. In choosing to be with Mal, I had to watch them get older and eventually pass."

A lump forms in my throat. "Did you tell them about Mal?"

"Yes. I wasn't sure if I should, but the alternative was disappearing from their lives. Perhaps watching them from afar. In the end, it was Mal who convinced me to tell them. They didn't believe me at first, so Mal transformed in front of them."

I laugh. "I bet that convinced them."

"Yes."

"Did you ever regret giving up your mortality for as long as you did?"

"No. Never. It was hard and heartbreaking at times, but the love we felt for each other made it worth it." She puts her hand over mine. "I can tell you the secret to having forever with Brin if you want to know."

I frown. "I got the impression Brin didn't have the power to extend anyone's life. I assumed it's because he's half human."

She shakes her head. "I told him he couldn't extend my life. He can extend yours."

"I—don't understand."

She sighs, beckons me closer, and drops her voice to a whisper. "The secret is sex."

I widen my eyes.

"Demon seed, to be precise. It has life-extending properties. Don't ask me how or why."

"Demon magic. Got it. Demon seed, huh? Wow."

"That's why I'm telling you and not my son. It was awkward enough having the birds and the bees conversation with him without trying to explain how he can extend the life of his lover." She squeezes my hand. "I'm trusting you with this information. Please don't use it to hurt Brin."

"I would never, ever do anything to hurt him."

She smiles. "You're a good man, Nurse Ian. Thank you for saving Brin."

"I'd do it again in a heartbeat. I love him. I want to be with him."

"Forever?"

My heart skips a beat.

"It's not a decision you need to make now. You have the information you need if you want to take that step. Also, remember it's not permanent. It didn't take long for me to start ageing again after Mal was taken from me." She looks at the door. "How long do you think it will take Brin to find me a good cup of tea?"

I chuckle. "No idea, but at least you know it'll be the perfect temperature when he gives it to you."

Her eyes sparkle. "Yes, it will."

Mother was home from hospital for all of five minutes before she asked Ian to show her how to summon Father. It was something she wanted to do alone, which stung a little, so it's a good thing I have Ian to hold me while we wait downstairs.

I can't sit still. I keep getting up and pacing the room. Every time I walk past Ian, he grabs my hand, pulls me onto his knee, and distracts me with kisses.

It's been a week since he rescued me from hell. A week in which I've craved him more than ever. While he doesn't have a magical dick capable of erasing the memory of my short stint in hell, being close to him has definitely helped me feel safe and secure.

While Ian worked, I visited Mother. Afterwards, Ian showed me the local area. He's booked time off to take me farther afield. Everything I've seen so far has been exciting, beautiful, and wonderful. But when it comes to deciding where to go or what to see next, I'm like a kid in a sweet shop wanting to sample everything but not knowing where to start.

On the plus side, there haven't been any demons sniffing around. So maybe, hopefully, the disembodied voice has kept his word.

"Why is it taking so long?" I ask as Ian pulls me onto his knee for what's probably the hundredth time.

"Do you have any idea how often I had to repeat the incantation and call your name?"

"No. How many times?"

Ian laughs and shrugs. "I lost count. A lot."

"But you didn't give up."

"No." He lifts my necklace with one finger and fans it against my skin. "Giving up was never an option. My boy needed me to save him."

I press the back of my hand against my forehead and pretend to swoon. "My hero." I kiss him. "Thank you for rescuing me. Although my plan would have worked eventually."

"Singing annoying songs badly until the Devil got sick of you and threw you out of hell?"

I grin. "Exactly. It was a foolproof plan."

"My plan worked faster."

"It did."

"I've never been more grateful for the internet."

I chuckle. "The internet is a wonderful invention." I snap my head up as footsteps creak above us. "Is that—? Do you think—?"

"There's only one way to find out."

We stand and, holding hands, leave the reception room and dart up the stairs, just as Mother exits her bedroom. She's not alone. Father is behind her. They are holding hands as tightly as Ian and I are. Mother looks different. Rejuvenated. Her eyes sparkle with a vigour they haven't in years. Her back is straighter, and she's not using her cane. I tilt my head, curiosity almost getting the better of me, before I decide I don't want or need to know.

"Brin," Father says. "It's good to see you again."

I fold my arms. "I hope you didn't doubt that Mother would save you."

He chuckles. "Not for one moment."

"I'm sorry it took so long," Mother says. "I got old while you were waiting for me."

Father turns to her and caresses her cheek. "You are still the most beautiful woman I've ever known, and I am still hopelessly in love with you."

Mother sniffs. "I love you too."

"Thank you for protecting our son all these years." They kiss, and then Father turns to Ian. "And you're the man who inspired Brin to tell Lucifer he was wrong about love."

Ian raises his eyebrows. "I—am?" He gives me a questioning look.

My cheeks get hot. "Was that Lucifer?" I ask in an innocent tone. "I'm still convinced he was a jumped-up prison guard."

Ian's mouth drops open. "You said that? To Lucifer?"

"He did. And a lot of other things. Brin is very spirited."

I shrug and smile. "I prefer chaotic."

Ian hugs me to him. "Chaotic and brave."

I make a strangled noise. "Brave. Crazy. Reckless. They're all synonyms, right?"

Ian chuckles. "Not quite."

"Will you be staying, Father?"

"I wouldn't want to be anywhere else. I belong with Martha. I always have and always will."

"Which means you don't have to feel guilty about running off and exploring the world with Ian," Mother says. "And you should. You've been cooped up for far too long, sweetheart. Enjoy your newfound freedom. Spread your wings and fly."

"Literally or figuratively?" I ask.

She laughs. "If you can find somewhere no one will see you do it, why not literally?"

I swing Ian's hand. "What do you reckon? Do you want to come flying with me?"

"Are you strong enough to carry me?"

I flex my arm muscle. "I'm stronger than I look."

IT'S DARK. Millions of stars hang in the cloudless sky. The moon is full, the air is crisp, and it's a perfect night for flying.

"Paragliders launch themselves off here." Ian claps his hands.

I stretch my wings. "Do you want me to make sure I can still fly before taking you with me, Daddy?"

He puts his hands on my waist and pecks my lips. "I trust you, boy."

I grimace. "I haven't even tried to fly since I was a child."

"You can do it. I believe in you."

"You didn't clap."

Ian frowns and then laughs. "You're not a fairy."

"Demon. Fairy. Close enough. If only I had fairy dust. I know, you could sprinkle me in cum. That's close enough, right?"

Ian laughs harder and shakes his head. "I love you. You can do this."

I roll my shoulders back and flex my wings. "I can."

He holds my hand. "Ready?"

"Yes."

We run forward together and jump at the same time. My wings spread out behind me, catching the wind and carrying us upwards. I pull Ian against me. He wraps his arms around me, holding on tight as we soar above deserted fields. Well, they're not quite deserted. There are some very confused sheep down there.

"This is amazing!" I whoop for joy.

"It is. A little terrifying but also amazing."

"I've got you, Daddy."

He rests his head on my shoulder. "I know you do, boy. And I've got you."

"Happy anniversary, boy," Ian says in a low, sexy tone.

I'm lying on my stomach on our bed, with my chin on my folded arms, staring at the most amazing view. No, not Ian, although he is the best view ever, especially when he's naked. The Eiffel Tower.

It's been three years since Ian almost fucked me on a sheet-covered sofa at Nethermire House. Three amazing years, if you skip the part where Mother ended up in the hospital and I got dragged to hell.

I touch my day collar and smile. We've seen and done so much since Ian freed me. We toured the length and breadth of the UK, seeing everything on and off the beaten path. We visited the Angkor temples, the Great Barrier Reef, Machu Picchu, the Grand Canyon, the Colosseum in Rome and dozens more amazing places. But we both fell in love with Paris so much that we moved here three months ago. I miss Mother, but she has Father to keep her company now. Thanks to him, she's vibrant and full of life once more, and they are still very much in love.

I spend most of my days in my human form, but I don't mind anymore. Ian knows what I truly am, and when we're alone, I get to be myself if I want to be. He doesn't mind either way. He takes me as I am, whether that's a naughty demon or a needy human. Right now, I'm mostly human. I haven't altered my eyes or made my horns disappear.

"Happy anniversary, Daddy."

He runs his finger up and down my spine. "I love you."

I giggle. "I know that. You tell me about one hundred times every day." I lean across and peck his lips. "What are we going to do for our anniversary? Aside from having sex. That's a given. In fact, maybe that's all we need to do. Make love all day long."

"Hm, that sounds like a good plan. But first, I have a gift for you."

"Aw, you shouldn't have."

"I like spoiling you."

"I know. But the only present I have to give you is myself."

"There's something else you can give me."

I frown. "What, Daddy?"

"An answer."

I deepen my frown. "An answer?"

He nods, reaches across the bed to his bedside drawer, and pulls out a small box. He opens it and shows me the contents. A ring. It's a plain band, the colour of which shifts from silver to flame red as he moves it in the light.

"I adore you, boy. Will you be mine?" He stares into my eyes. "Forever."

My chest tightens. "Forever? I'd love to, Daddy. But I can't— I don't know how to—" I blink tears.

He puts his finger over my lips. "I happen to know how Mal stopped Martha from ageing."

"You do? How come you know and I don't? How long have you known?"

Ian chuckles. "It wasn't a conversation Martha wanted to have with you. She told me while she was in hospital when she sent you searching for tea."

I remember. I got hopelessly lost and even more distracted and got back to the hospital two hours later. At least I found good tea. There was a little stall on the market that sold about two hundred different blends. I shake my head, bringing myself back to the moment.

"Why couldn't Mother tell me?"

Ian twirls his finger over my shoulder. "She was embarrassed and thought you would be too."

"I'm so confused."

"Cum."

"Come? Now I'm even more confused."

He trails his hand down my back, around my hip, and under my body to palm my cock. "Cum."

I widen my eyes. "Seriously?"

"Yes."

I roll onto my back and stare at the ceiling. "So, what? I fuck you, fill you with cum, and you live forever?"

"Something like that. Except, as you already know, it won't last."

"So I'd have to fuck you regularly?"

Ian shrugs.

"Why are you telling me now? You've known for what? Two and a half years?"

"About that." Ian sighs. "I needed to be sure. It's not an easy decision to make, Brin. I'll keep reinventing myself. Change jobs, move homes, find new friends. Then there's my family—"

I roll onto my side and cup his jaw. "I'd never ask you to give them up."

He turns his face to kiss my palm. "I know, boy."

"We could tell them about me. Maybe not explain that my cum is going to make you immortal."

"Let's not tell them that."

I stroke his beard. "Do you truly want to be with me forever, Daddy?"

"Yes, boy, as long as you want it too."

"I do. You're mine. I'm yours."

"So, what's your answer?" He waves the box from side to side.

"Yes."

Grinning, he takes the ring out of the box and slides it onto my finger.

We cuddle up to each other, my cheek pressed against his furry chest. "About the magic demon cum thing—"

"Hm?"

"I'll get used to topping. I'll do anything for you."

Ian kisses my head. "You don't have to top me if you don't want to, boy."

"Um, I sort of have to."

Ian arches an eyebrow. "Do you? There's more than one way to fill me with your cum."

"There is?"

He grins, pushes me onto my back, and moves down the bed so he can nuzzle my cock with his mouth.

"Oh! There is!" Why didn't I think of that?

It's not as if Ian hasn't gone down on me before. It's one of many ways he enjoys making me come. He doesn't swallow often. He likes pulling his mouth off right before I orgasm so he can collect my cum in his hand and use it as lube. Plus, it's more usual for me to suck him off. I adore feasting on his cock.

"How often do you think I'll have to give you blow jobs to stay forty-eight forever?"

"Hm, I don't know." There is no way I'm going to ask him if Mother gave him the answer to that question, not when he's nibbling his way along my dick. "Maybe every day?"

He smiles at me, his gaze radiating affection. "Drinking your cum on a daily basis is going to be such a hardship."

I snort. "Yeah, I bet it will be."

"But I'll do it," he says in a mock solemn tone. "So we can be together forever."

"Think of all the things we could do."

"Why don't you come up with a list, boy? And we'll tick them off one at a time."

"The world's most epic bucket list?"

He chuckles. "Something like that."

"I will, Daddy. But do you know what will be at the top of the list every single day?"

"Me sucking your cock?"

I rake my teeth over my lower lip. "Aside from that."

"What?"

"Kissing you. Running my fingers through your chest hair. Cuddling you. Talking to you. Making love to you."

"That's five things, boy."

"Nah. They all boil down to one thing."

"Oh?"

"Being your boy."

AUTHOR'S NOTE

Apparently, I like writing bratty, self-assured boys who aren't afraid to tell their Daddy what they want. Felix (*A Boy Made of Sunshine*) and Barney (*A Silver Fox for Kinkmas*) are also good examples of this type of character. In fact, I think Felix, Barney, and Brin would get along well.

Fun fact, when I first started coming up with ideas for this story, I'd intended on having a demon Daddy and a human boy. I knew the boy would have to have a bratty or bad boy streak (have you seen the gorgeous cover model?), but I wasn't envisaging him being the demon until I saw a beautiful drawing of a demon, and all my ideas got flipped on their head.

It's funny how a single image can change everything. Getting side-tracked for a second, that's probably why I've written a lot of artist characters (that and I'd love to be able to draw and paint!).

Getting back on track, Brin was fun and refreshing to write. I loved writing a character who wanted—no, needed—to be accepted for being their true, authentic self. And, of course, Ian is the Daddy who is capable of doing just that.

To wrap this up, I'd like to thank Ashlynn Mills for inviting me into the *Possessive Love* series.

Thanks also go to my alpha readers, Leanne and Lauren, and everyone who supports me on Patreon (www.patreon.com/colette davison), including Miriam, Danielle, Gianni, Lisa, Colleen, Kay, Lauren, Tamara, Wendy, Beth, Emma, Guin, Helen, Trish, Tammy, and Vicki.

Thank you for reading *Recalling His Demon*. I hope you enjoyed Brin and Ian's story.

I you'd like to connect with me, please sign up for my newsletter (www.colettedavison.com/newsletter) or join me in my Facebook reader group, *Colette Davison's Cosy Corner* (facebook.com/groups/colettescosycorner).

ALSO BY COLETTE DAVISON

SERIES:

Why I...

Why I Left You (Book 1) - hurt/comfort, second chance

Why I Need You (Book 2) - hurt/comfort, insta dad

Why I Trust You (Book 3) - hurt/comfort, long distance relationship

Omnibus edition

Love on Pointe

A Dance For Two (Boosk 1) - stepbrothers, hurt/comfort; listen on Audible

A Dance For You (Book 2) - age-gap, forbidden romance; listen on Audible

Omnibus edition

Heaven and Hell Club

Unbreakable (prequel) - fake boyfriend, size difference

Broken (Book 1) - hurt/comfort, age-gap; listen on Audible

Wicked (FREE short story)

Forgotten (Book 2) - hurt/comfort, disabled MC; listen on Audible

Forgiven (Book 3) - hurt/comfort, bisexual awakening; listen on Audible

Chasing Gold

Hold Me Up (Book 1) - second chance, hurt/comfort

Don't Hold Back (Book 2) - rivals to lovers, grumpy and sunshine, hurt/comfort

Offbeat Shifters

Secretly Mine (Book 1) - alternative universe, shifters, age-gap, pop star

Openly Yours (Book 2) - alternate universe, shifters, age-gap, hurt/comfort

Unapologetically Me (Book 3) - alternate universe, shifters, age-gap, personal redemption

Unashamedly Us (Book 4) - alternate universe, shifters, age-gap, mpreg

The Alphabet of Desire

A is for Aftercare (Book 1) - age-gap, BDSM, boss/employee, sensory play

B is for Beg (Book 2) - MMM, age-gap, Daddy kink, interracial relationship

C is for Comfort (Book 3) - age-gap, Daddy kink, single dad

My Kinky Housemate

My Kinky Housemate (prequel) - kitten play, old friends to lovers

Sugar Bunny (Book 1) - age-gap, MMM, D/switch/s, bunny play, BDSM

Plaything (Book 2) - kinky role play, breath play, hurt/comfort

Collar Me (Book 3) - puppy play, handcuffs, fantasy toy

Keep Me On Edge (Book 4) - edging, pain play, hurt/comfort

Awakened Desires (Book 5) - sensory play, slow burn, bisexual awakening

Camboy (Book 6) - MMMM, D/D/s/s, age-gap, spanking

Cuffd

Dear Daddy, Please Hold Us - MMM, Daddy kink, age-play; listen on Audible

Greeking Out - long distance friends to lovers, Daddy kink, age play; listen on Audible

His Boy to Cherish - Daddy kink, age-play, disabled Daddy, ABDL; listen on Audible

Crazy Little Thing Cold Love - Daddy kink, age-gap, hurt/comfort; listen on Audible

A Silver Fox for Kinkmas - Daddy kink, May to December, spankings, orgasm denial; listen on Audible

STANDALONES:

Contemporary Romance

I Wished For You - MMM, friends to lovers; listen on Audible

What Works For Us - age-gap, role-play, Daddy kink; listen on Audible

A Boy Made Of Sunshine - grumpy and sunshine, Daddy kink; listen on Audible

Take the Plunge - best friend's brother, grumpy/sunshine, forced proximity

Lessons in Chemistry - MMM, slow burn, nerd/jock/slacker, first times, fake date

Praising Haru - praise kink, opposites attract, 6-year age-gap

Paranormal Romance

Beyond the Surface - fairy tale retelling, insta love, fated mates

Run Free - alternate universe, shifters, mpreg

Recalling My Demon - Daddy kink, age-gap

For You I Fall (with T.N. Nova) - hurt/comfort, age-gap

Novellas

One Room At The Inn - MMM, close proximity

Oblivious - friends to lovers, double bi-sexual awakening, no angst, lots of cupcakes; listen on Audible

Getting Signed - best friend's brother, make-up, opposites attract

Short Stories

Secret Holiday Kisses - Christmas in July, dad's best friend, age-gap

A Boy Full of Pumpkins - Halloween, grumpy and sunshine, Daddy kink, audio available for $5+ Patrons to download.

ABOUT THE AUTHOR

Colette's personal love story began at university, where she met her future husband. An evening of flirting, in the shadow of Lancaster castle, eventually led to a fairytale wedding. She's enjoying her own 'happy ever after' in the north of England with her husband, two beautiful children and her writing.

You can connect with Colette in the following ways:

Website: www.colettedavison.com
Facebook group: www.facebook.com/groups/colettescosycorner/
Mailing list: www.colettedavison.com/newsletter
Patreon: www.patreon.com/colettedavison
Sticker store: https://colette-davison.sumup.link/

 facebook.com/ColetteDavisonAuthor

 x.com/Colette_Davison

 instagram.com/colettedavison

 bookbub.com/profile/colette-davison

.

Printed in Poland
by Amazon Fulfillment
Poland Sp. z o.o., Wrocław

35116370R00104